determined to protect
Edmund from danger

She hadn't reckoned on Jason. The dog gave a yelp of delight and launched himself towards the invalid's bed, only to be brought up short by Ravensworth, who caught his collar and, with one swift jerk, pulled him away from his nephew.

"Leave him alone, you brute!" shrieked Theodora.

"Don't be alarmed, Miss Waverton," Ravensworth said. "He has not hurt me."

"Not him! You!" raged Theodora.

"My leg! Don't let him go!" moaned Edmund from the bed.

"Jason is just very...very friendly," Theodora tried to explain, turning to Ravensworth. "I must have forgotten to bolt the stable door. I saw your horse, so naturally I was in a hurry."

"You can't imagine how flattered I am," rejoined Edmund's guardian. "I had no idea my presence was so pleasing to you."

Regency England: 1811-1820

"It was the best of times, it was the worst of times...."

As George III languished in madness, the pampered and profligate Prince of Wales led the land in revelry and the elegant Beau Brummel set the style. Across the Channel, Napoleon continued to plot against the English until his final exile to St. Helena. Across the Atlantic, America renewed hostilities with an old adversary, declaring war on Britain in 1812. At home, Society glittered, love matches abounded and poets such as Lord Byron flourished. It was a time of heroes and villains, a time of unrelenting charm and gaiety, when entire fortunes were won or lost on a turn of the dice and reputation was all. A dazzling period that left its mark on two continents and whose very name became a byword for elegance and romance.

Books by Petra Nash

HARLEQUIN REGENCY ROMANCE
36—LADY HARRIET'S HARVEST

Don't miss any of our special offers. Write to us at the following address for information on our newest releases.

Harlequin Reader Service
P.O. Box 1397, Buffalo, NY 14240
Canadian address: P.O. Box 603,
Fort Erie, Ont. L2A 5X3

MR. RAVENSWORTH'S WARD

PETRA NASH

Harlequin Books

TORONTO • NEW YORK • LONDON
AMSTERDAM • PARIS • SYDNEY • HAMBURG
STOCKHOLM • ATHENS • TOKYO • MILAN
MADRID • WARSAW • BUDAPEST • AUCKLAND

Published March 1993

ISBN 0-373-31193-1

MR. RAVENSWORTH'S WARD

CHAPTER ONE

A WISP OF SMOKE rose from the chimney of the cottage. As she knocked at the door, Theodora Allendale reflected sadly that it might more correctly be called a hut, or a hovel. The cob walls that formed the two small rooms sagged alarmingly, propped up here and there with lumps of timber. Of that, at least, there could be no shortage, she thought, in the middle of the Ashdown Forest.

There was a listening silence within, and Theodora, ignoring the icy trickle of air that crept with a nasty viciousness through and under her cloak, leaching away the warmth that brisk walking had engendered, patiently knocked again.

"It's all right, Mag. It's me, Miss Theo," she called ungrammatically. She was rewarded by the sound of wordless grumbling, and a slow shuffle of footsteps. Hefting her basket, that seemed to grow in weight with some kind of monstrous mathematical progression, Theodora composed her face and waited imperturbably. The door opened a crack, revealing no more than a bright, suspicious eye, and four gnarled, dark-stained fingers.

"Well?" The voice was not welcoming. Theodora hid a sigh, and smiled brightly.

"Good day, Mag."

The eye was not appeased. Nor did the door open any further.

"'Tisn't right. 'Tisn't proper. To call me out of me name, and her no more'n a mawk."

Theodora tried another tactic, and adopted the voice and accent of the village.

"I do beg yer pardon, surelye, Mistress Mag." The door opened a little further, and the old woman stood revealed in layer upon layer of greyish homespun garments.

"Adone do with that talk, Miss Theodora. I dunna-many times as I've called over you for that. 'Tisn't fitten, a gurt girl like you be, and so I tell you."

"Now, don't be cross with me, when I've walked all this way to visit you! Aren't you pleased to see me?"

Mag gave an unlovely sniff.

"I suppose as you'll have to come in. Mind you don't spannel dirt over my floor, now."

Obediently Theodora wiped her feet on the square of sacking, and followed her unwilling hostess into the cottage. It was dark, after the bright winter afternoon, but spotlessly clean, smelling of the herbs hung in bunches to dry, and of the wood fire. Lifting the basket on to the table, Theodora began to unpack it.

"What's all this, then?" The old lady looked disparagingly on the contents. "An't no call for charity here, miss."

"This," said Theodora, placidly laying down a pot of preserves, "is not charity. This is a gift from my mother, as one neighbour to another. And I am to tell you, she would be grateful for more of your herb tea, and some ointment for Cook's scalded hand, if you can spare it."

For the first time the old lady's face softened.

"Ah, a real lady she be, your mother, and never one to gridgen of what she has. That her own wine, is it?"

"Yes, and I helped make it, and the preserves, too."

"Best sit down, then, while I look out the ointment. Burnt bad, be she? When did she catch hurt?"

"The day before yesterday. It's very sore. The kettle slipped, and splashed her."

"Hm. She always were one for a boffle, that Em'ly. You'll take a sup of tea? The kettle's just abouten boiled."

"Real tea, or Donkey tea? You know I don't mind—I'm not one of your dentical fine ladies!"

"When did I ever give you aught but real, less it was my herb tea? Donkey tea, indeed! A good bannicking, that's what you deserves!"

"But I like Donkey tea! I didn't mean to be rude, Mag. Don't be vexed with me!"

"Well, then." Theodora could see she was mollified. Tea made from pounded burnt toast was not uncommon in poor houses, and Mag, long widowed, was very poor. February was a hard month for such people, when there was nothing to be gathered in woodland or hedgerow, and precious stores must be relied on. Mag stubbornly continued to live where she had always done, in the house built by her charcoal-burner husband, miles from any village.

The charcoal-burners of the forest had always been a race apart, and in recent times when there was little call for their product their number had dwindled. Many had moved to farms or villages and taken other work, but Mag said she was too old to change, and she would stay as she was for the few years left to her. Such solitary existence, and her knowledge of herbal medicines, had led to her being feared by local villagers, and, if it had not been for Theodora's mother, she must long since have given up, or perished.

Theodora drank her tea, and obediently ate a piece of the "plum heavy" she was given.

"Will you read my tea-leaves?" she asked hopefully.

"Be blamed if I will. That's no more than heathen nonsense, as I've told you afore."

"Read my hand, then?"

Mag sniffed, but she took the regrettably grubby paw held out to her, and studied it carefully.

"You still biting your nailses? Tell your mother to paint 'em with bitter aloes. Give you some cream, I will, too. Proper rough, they be, real slommaky."

"That's not what I meant! Oh, please do. You always said you'd do it when I was grown-up, and I am, nearly."

The piercing eyes looked her up and down. The small, slender figure, newly rounded into womanhood and as yet uncertain in its movement, going from grace to coltish clumsiness and back again. The hair, thick and curling, its rich chestnut catching fire from the glowing embers on the hearth. The eyes, wide and limpid beneath arched brows and thick brown lashes, so deeply blue that they looked violet in the dim light. Unaware of her own beauty, Theodora looked back, and had the sense to keep her silence.

"Give me your hand again." Even the voice seemed different, more rounded, more commanding. Obediently Theodora held out her hand to Mag who, risen, seemed suddenly much bigger than before. Mag looked down at the palm, then folded her own hands over the one she held.

"It is good," she said.

"What is? My future? Oh, do tell me, please. Shall I travel? Cross the sea? Fall in love? Marry, and have babies?"

"That? Let be how 'twill. First, you must know yourself."

"Know myself? I don't understand. Of course I know myself." There was no answer. Theodora looked down at her hands, blushing. "You mean, who I am? I know that, don't I?"

"There's no more to be said. Never be frouden, child. I told you, it is good." She would say no more, and grew irritable when Theodora pressed her, packing up the herbs and the jar of ointment in a piece of old linen and almost pushing Theodora out of the door. The girl was disappointed, but not worried. She had hoped for romance and

a fairy tale of handsome young men, and instead received
only cryptic advice, but she soon put it out of her mind.
She had known Mag all her life, had spent many a happy
childhood hour helping her husband to build his clamp of
wood, or to sort the charcoal when the clamp was un-
made—charcoal of the kind which had once smelted iron
for Plantagenet and Tudor cannon and shot. To have old
Mag look at her hand was no more than a game, like peel-
ing an apple in one piece and throwing the rind over one's
shoulder to see if it made a letter.

Her feet as light as her heart, Theodora passed swiftly
along the woodland track that would bring her, eventu-
ally, to the small but commodious house in the depths of
the Ashdown Forest which had been her home, and her
mother's, for as long as she could remember. The thin
February sunlight had never attained enough warmth to
soften the ice-hard ground, or melt the crackling skin of ice
that covered the puddles. Pockets of frost lay white and
sparkling in every hollow and shadow, and the air was
crystal-sharp. Warmly wrapped in a woollen shawl under
the shabby cloak that enveloped her small figure, Theodora was sublimely indifferent to the cold which brought,
did she but know it, a glow of colour to her cheeks and
lips, and a sparkle to her eyes.

Not for her the thin muslins and dampened petticoats of
high fashion. Her simple, high-waisted gown was of ser-
viceable dimity, and her stockings and petticoats warmly
made of fine wool. Her basket swung in one hand, which
was slipped through an opening in her cloak and warm in
its neatly mended glove, and the other clasped the cloak
firmly around her. No need, today, to worry about lifting
her skirts clear of the mud.

Allowed by her mother, unusually for one of her station, to roam the countryside with no more protection than
a dog, nothing irked her more than to be compelled to stay

indoors when the sun was shining. Today she had not even brought her dog, since Mag made no secret of her dislike of him. Her errand done, her small gifts received, because she was known and came without condescension, she made her way home. It was growing late, the sun was already huge and red in the winter sky, but Theodora knew this path as if it had been her own back garden, and her mother was not given to undue worrying. Nor was Theodora subject to imagining ghosts or highwaymen behind every shadowed bush. She was an alarmingly practical young woman.

So she made her way along the path in perfect contentment. She was, regrettably, whistling, an unfeminine skill taught her at an early age by a boon companion, the gardener's boy. Her mother deplored such habits, and pointed out that what was—just—permissible in a tomboy of seven, with gappy teeth, was scarcely allowable in a young lady of the mature age of almost eighteen. To which Theodora had cheerfully agreed, and obligingly confined such musical exploits to moments when she was sure of complete solitude.

Her disobedience to her mother's behest was her undoing. Absorbed in a spirited rendering of "Over the Hills and Far Away," as it appeared in *The Beggar's Opera,* she swirled round a corner in the path, only to find that her flying cloak was caught and firmly held by a recalcitrant thorn bush. To jerk it, and risk tearing the cloth which, though worn, was still sound and good, was unthinkable. She therefore laid down her basket and drawing as close as she could to the bush to give herself as much play as possible, began to unhook the fabric.

It was anxious work, and her fingers were cold; moreover, the sun was by now casting little more than a dull glow, so she had to work by feel alone. So absorbed was she in her task, that she quite failed to take notice of the sound of hoofbeats, muffled in the thick layer of fallen leaves which carpeted the side of the track, that was steadily approaching.

It was not until the horse, at a steady canter, swept round the bend that she became aware of it. If she had kept still all would have been well, for her brown cloak, faded in places, merged with the background of earth, tree-trunk and bush, and she was almost invisible in the gathering dusk. Surprise, however, made her turn her head, and the sudden movement, together with the flash of white that was her face within her hood, caused the horse to shy, dancing sideways across the rutted track.

The rider, with a curse, controlled his mount with apparent ease, though when it finally came to rest, sidling nervously nearer as if still half inclined to bolt, she saw the muscles taut and hard in his arms and hands. She was not herself a rider, having had little occasion to learn in their straitened, horseless household, but she had often watched the local hunt meet, and she knew good riding when she saw it.

Her instinctive movement away from the restless horse had hooked her cloak further into the thorns, and she was now almost inextricably entangled. She struggled to unfasten it, wanting to present her apologies properly, but was forestalled. The horse, still skittering but under firm control, came ever nearer, and a strong hand, impeccably gloved in York tan, reached down and twitched the hood from her head. Unable to move, Theodora kept still and looked up.

It was a sight that silenced her, cutting short her immediate protest, and leaving her wide-eyed and staring. Never before had such an elegant being been seen in the depths of the Ashdown Forest. From the crown of his smoothly brushed beaver hat to the refulgently gleaming boot that was conveniently near to her fascinated gaze, he was quite obviously a nonpareil, a Pink of the Ton. No country tailor had set his hand to the many-caped coat that sat so elegantly over the shoulders, which obviously had no need of padding to give them the required shape, being already broad and strongly muscled. Buckskin breeches were moulded without crease or wrinkle to his strong legs, and his face... She became aware that she had been staring, *bouche bée*, and closed her mouth, dropping her eyes in confusion.

"Well, well, what have we here? A rustic beauty?" His careless drawl brought the colour to her cheeks in an angry rush. She raised her eyes again, and wished that she had not. A pair of disconcertingly piercing hazel eyes under strongly marked brows looked quizzically down from a clean-shaven, uncompromisingly craggy face. A slight smile, that did nothing to engender confidence in her, lifted the corners of his mouth, displaying strong, even teeth.

She opened her lips to tell him that she was no rustic, but Miss Theodora Allendale of Chelwood Cottage, then closed them again with a snap, discovering within herself a strong reluctance to have him know who she was. With characteristic stubbornness she kept her eyes raised to his, and saw the smile deepen and reach his eyes. It was very attractive, and she fought to keep back her answering smile, feeling sure that he knew just what effect he was likely to have on the average female. Well, he should not cozen her! The horse, quiet now, dropped its head to snuff hopefully in her empty basket.

"Little Red Riding Hood, out of uniform?" he suggested. "Did your grandmama not warn you about wolves, my dear?" She did not answer, meeting his teasing look austerely.

"It would have been a shame if I had passed without seeing you, of course," he continued in an equable tone, "but was it really necessary to startle the horse? In these icy conditions we could well have slipped, you know. A broken limb or two is no more than tribute to your beauty, from me, but it is unfair to expect the horse to see it that way."

Rightly dismissing this as an attempt to provoke her into speech, Theodora kept her eyes resolutely fixed on his, refusing to respond either to his banter or the lurking twinkle in those disturbing hazel eyes. She resumed, by feel, her ineffectual tugging at the cloak, which seemed impossibly caught round the branches.

His feet kicked free of the stirrups, and next moment he had dismounted, looping his reins over his arm. He was even taller than she had thought, over six feet, and her diminutive stature meant that the top of her head came level with one of the large silver buttons on his coat. His hands closed gently over hers.

"A rustic beauty in distress, I now see," he murmured in a conversational tone. "Hold still, Phoebe, and I will slay the wolf—or is it a dragon?" His strong fingers closed round the branch that held her, snapping off the twigs one by one until she was able to move away from the tree. Taken separately, the twigs abandoned that semblance of malignant vitality that made it seem as though they clutched the fabric with a will of their own, and were easier to disentangle. Soon the last of them was flicked away into the undergrowth.

Theodora was suddenly aware of his large, disturbing nearness. She was reluctant to betray her unease by moving away, so she kept her head down, her fingers idly playing with a small rent which, in spite of his care, had appeared in the material of the cloak.

"Come, now, my girl, where is your gratitude? Dragon slaying does not come cheap, you know."

Theodora hung her head, bobbed a country child's curtsy, and mumbled a few words of thanks in a low voice. She was only too aware that in the old, unfashionable cloak, with the shawl that crossed her chest and was tied behind her for extra warmth, she looked like any village girl. She could only hope that he would take her for such, and not tease her any more. Living as retired as they did, she was not likely ever to see him again, since he must be staying in one of the great houses of the neighbourhood.

His eyes ran swiftly over her, noting the white skin that had obviously been protected from sun and wind, and had never worked out of doors; the gloves which, though frequently and carefully mended, were of fine kid; the glimpse of snowy lace-trimmed cambric that showed at her wrist and neck.

"Speak up, girl! I cannot hear you!"

She responded with a few words in the language and accent of her old crony, the gardener's boy. In the past her mother had scolded her for copying him; now Theodora was glad of the accomplishment.

"Beg your pardon, sir, surelye. And right grateful I be too, sir. You made a proper job with my cloak on them old thornses." Her eyes looked guilelessly up into his, and dropped. He raised a hand to cover, for a moment, his twitching lips.

"Come, now, my dear, I expect something better than that! If not your hand and heart, for which I have little use, then at least your pretty lips!" To her horror and amazement she found herself firmly held by one muscular arm round her waist. She was frozen with surprise and embarrassment, and before she could do more than gasp his other hand was at her neck, thumb and fingers caressing the line of jaw and cheek as he lifted her face. He was so close that she could smell the aroma of Russia leather that came from him, a not unpleasant but utterly masculine scent that seemed to surround her as his lips came down on hers. They were firm and demanding. The only embraces she had ever known, from her mother or her mother's few friends, had never been like this. They had been soft, on cheek or lips or brow. This was fierce and sudden, sending a tingle of awareness that was almost painful in its intensity down her spine.

To her horror she found that she was enjoying this new sensation. She recoiled, brought up short by that hard arm. He lifted his face to look down at her.

"Very enjoyable. I think I must insist on full payment for my help. How many twigs was it?" His lips again sought hers.

Unable to speak or to break free, and working on the principle that actions spoke louder than words, she drew back her foot and gave him a hearty kick. Her feet were shod not in the fine kid half-boots that befitted her station, but in sturdy leather, the soles well studded by the village cobbler so that she had no need to fear mud or ice. Though her stature might be diminutive, her muscles were strongly developed by walking and gardening, and she had the satisfaction of seeing him wince at the blow.

"Little vixen!" She drew back her foot for a second kick, but swiftly moving his grip he took her by the elbows, lifting her bodily and swinging her away from him to the middle of the path.

"If you'll not stay to be kissed, you'd best be off," he said, speeding her on her way with a neat slap, as if she had been a small child. Gathering the rags of her dignity around her, Theodora returned to pick up her basket, keeping a wary eye on him where he stood quietening his horse, which was restless again after the flurry of movement. With a cursty which she hoped might convey ironical disdain, she walked slowly away, head held high, footsteps unhurried. Once round the corner of the path, however, she abandoned all dignity and fled, cloak billowing unheeded around her, down the darkening track and through the winding paths that led to home.

He watched her leave, a small smile playing at the corners of his mouth. He had in no way been deceived by her little act; for one thing, many village maidens would have welcomed the advances of someone of his obvious wealth. His kisses would have been returned with some enthusiasm, and he would undoubtedly have been expected to pay handsomely for them too. No rustic beauty he had ever met had attempted to do him injury, as this girl had done, and he found himself thinking with some admiration that he would have a fine bruise to show for it. A remarkably pretty girl, too, and quick-witted in her innocent way. It would be too much to say that he hoped to meet her again; it was unlikely to happen, after all. He did not intend to spend more time in the Forest than he had to, and once his tiresome business was accomplished he would return to his accustomed haunts with some relief. For a moment he wondered whether to follow the girl home, and find out more about her, but a minute's reflection persuaded him that he could ill afford the time. After all, there were plenty of pretty girls in the world.

Theodora hurried on her way, listening as she went. She half feared to hear hoofbeats following; it had occurred, finally, to her innocent mind that village maidens accosted in dark and lonely places by fashionable bucks risked worse than a few kisses. But only the sound of his laughter, hateful in her ears, pursued her.

At first she was carried along by anger, pure and uncomplicated. How dared he treat her so? Whoever she was, village girl or whatever else he had taken her for, how dared he kiss her like that, and laugh at her? And he, by his dress and demeanour, a gentleman? But that was the problem: she knew nothing of men, gentlemen or otherwise, or next to nothing. Who had she met? The Vicar, elderly and kind, who had prepared her for her Confirmation, and who preached dry and interminable sermons and lived a solitary, dusty life with a devoted housekeeper and a study full of books. The gardener's boy, who had grown up and, bored with village life, enlisted in the army and gone to fight Napoleon. She had wept for him for a whole day, but now she could scarcely recall his face.

The lights of home were in sight, and she slowed her pace. It would not do to arrive red-faced and panting. Her body still churned with anger, and she paused to confront it, analyse it, as was her habit with strong emotions. She did not like what she saw, and shrank from it. Then, with her usual courage, looked again, and saw that her main anger was not against him, but herself, because she had enjoyed it. She could not deny that her lips still tingled from his kiss, and when she thought of it a quiver ran through her. Never before had her body betrayed her mind in this way, and now for the first time she was frightened.

Once indoors, the familiar atmosphere of cheerful calm, made up of the scent of beeswax and pot-pourri, of the measured tick of the hall clock, of her mother's voice calling a gentle greeting, wrapped her round. She felt the quivering leave her skin as her body relaxed and an unexpected rush of tears rose to her eyes. She whisked them away, and called back to her mother.

"I am sorry to be so late, Mama. I will just put off my cloak, and tidy my hair, and I will be with you."

If her mother wondered at this unwonted display of tidiness, she made no remark, and Theodora ran up to her room.

The cloak was soon shed, hung by long habit in its place, for they could not afford many servants, and Theodora was accustomed to care for her own things. She was glad, now, that there was no maid to fuss over her, to ask about

the ruffled hair or the tear-brightened eyes. Theodora
splashed cold water from a jug into a bowl on the wash-
stand, and sluiced her face vigorously, scrubbing at her lips
until they were stinging. Then, sitting before her mirror,
she took out the pins that held the heavy mass of her hair,
already slipping down, so that it fell loose, then dragged a
brush ruthlessly through it before pinning it up, rather
more tightly than before. Then she stayed, her movements arrested, and stared at her reflection.

It was not something she often did. Hitherto her life had
been busy, happy, full of small pleasures and old-
established family rituals, simple and satisfying. Now for
the first time, wondering, her fingers strayed up to touch
her lips, then snatched back as if they had been burned.

"Theodora Allendale. Theodora Allendale," she whispered. The words suddenly sounded strange, unfamiliar.
Even the face that she thought belonged to those names
swam, in the pool of candlelight, like that of a stranger.
Almost frightened, she summoned up the safest image she
could think of—her mother's face. Broad and fair, blue
eyes like her own but hair still golden, it was better known
than her own. She superimposed the image on the face in
the mirror. For the first time, she thought; We are not very
alike. Her mind shivered away from this idea. Plenty of
children resembled one parent more than the other. Maybe
she took after her father.

That was it. The thing that had lurked behind her fear.
Her father, whoever he was. In childhood she had accepted that she and her mother lived alone together.
Knowing few other people, they were sufficient to one another, and she had felt no lack, no empty place in her life.
Nor had she questioned the fact that her mother never
mentioned her husband's name, or spoke of him.

Lately, however, Theodora had found herself wondering. Her mother, dressing always in the lilac or purple of half-mourning, she assumed was a widow. With the burgeoning romanticism of adolescence, she had thought with pity that sorrow for him had sealed her lips, and out of delicacy she had refrained from questioning, not to open old wounds. Now, for the first time, she doubted the assumption.

Completely inexperienced, she had been profoundly shocked by her own response to a stranger's kisses. Could it be, she wondered, that her birth was not as she had thought it? Was there some taint, some weakness that she had inherited? Had her mother, still young now, been betrayed at an early age into some disastrous alliance? It was not uncommon, she knew, for village girls to be "in trouble," particularly after the haymaking or harvest celebrations. Such chance-born children, as they were called, were generally accepted philosophically by the family. But for women of their class, no such mistakes were allowed. Her mind cold with panic, Theodora thought of their isolation, the fact that she seemed to have no other family, no grandparents, uncles, or cousins. That they never went visiting, or received visits, or even letters, from outside the immediate area.

Was that what Mag had meant? If so, her future was cloudy. Who would marry the nameless child of a woman whose family had cast her off? She examined her face again. Was there some sign, perhaps, that she had never noticed? Had he, that hateful man, known somehow that she was a girl who might be kissed with impunity? She swallowed hard, blinking back another betraying rush of tears.

Theodora was not without courage. She was, she decided, still the same person, whatever her birth might be.

If she was to spend her life here, her mother's companion, then she was still luckier than many. It was getting late. Theodora lifted her chin, shook out her skirts as she rose, and walked downstairs to tell her mother a suitably expurgated version of the afternoon's events.

CHAPTER TWO

"MAMA?"

The woman known to her neighbours as Mrs. Allendale looked up from her writing desk, set where the morning sun could light and the heat of the fire could warm her. The abstracted frown that creased her still unlined brow was smoothed away, to be replaced by a fond look as her eyes fell on her only child. By nature she was reserved, and taught in a hard school to hide her feelings behind an impassive face, so that only for Theodora could that soft look appear.

Certainly the girl was a sight to gladden any mother's heart this morning. She had been unusually silent the previous evening, when she had returned from her visit to Mag, but Mrs. Allendale had merely put it down to fatigue from the cold walk. They had spent their evening in their accustomed fashion, taking turn to read aloud while the other sewed, and if her daughter's good-night kiss had been more clinging than usual, she had not noticed it. Neither of them ever ate much breakfast, and the first meal of the day was a short affair, hurried through so that both could get on with the business of the day.

Busy with her work, her mother realised suddenly that Theodora had taken unusual pains with her toilette that morning. The unruly mane of chestnut hair, that only yesterday, surely, had fallen down her back and tangled itself in her pinafore buttons, was neatly, even severely arranged. The plain gown of white muslin, the bosom mod-

estly obscured by a fichu, the sleeves long to the wrist and
ending with a chaste frill of the same material, was draped
with a shawl, for added warmth, and fell in soft, classical
folds, unmarred by fidgeting feet or hands.

It also occurred to her that her daughter's face was paler
than usual, and there were shadows under her eyes, making them larger and more violet-coloured than ever. Her
look of delicate slightness was belied, her mother knew, by
a healthy strength both of body and spirit. Not for Theodora the fear of cold, chill, or damp, and their attendant
miseries. Nor, perhaps more importantly, the fear of
other's disapproval, unkindness or cruelty. Life in this
sheltered harbour had never shown her anything but
kindness and indulgence, tempered by calm good sense.

Something, then, had occurred yesterday, when she had
been to visit old Mag. All she had said, on her return, was
that the old woman had been cross at first, but grateful for
the gifts, and that she had scolded Theodora for not taking more care of her nails. Well, it was not the first time
she had been told that, at any rate.

"Mama!" Her reverie was interrupted by Theodora's
repeated demand. An unusual tone in her daughter's voice
told her that this was to be no everyday communication.

"Yes, my dear, what is it? You know I want to finish this
story today, if I can."

"I'm sorry, Mama. It could wait until later..."

A glance at her daughter's pale cheeks and downcast
eyes told her that Theodora had somehow been nerving
herself to speak, would almost welcome a chance to postpone whatever it was. It was unlike her; generally she
rushed happily headlong into everything, never stopping
to weigh the consequences until it was too late, then apologising cheerfully and sincerely. In fact Theodora, with a
self-control that surprised even herself, had resolved not
to mention her worries, nor to question her mother, until

the following day. A night's sleep might, she had hoped, compose her nerves, and give her strength to hear what her mother might tell her.

Mrs. Allendale laid down her pen, and pushed the paper resolutely away from her.

"No time like the present, dear child."

Still her daughter hesitated, not looking up at her mother.

"Mama, would you say I am a woman grown now?"

Mrs. Allendale looked at the softly rounded figure, from which the simple home-made gown could not detract, and the face whose childish curves had lately fined down to more elegant planes that revealed the good bones beneath. Aware of her scrutiny, the cheeks took on a tinge of colour.

"Am I, Mama?" she persisted.

"Yes, my dear, I would say you are." Her mother's voice was both proud and rueful, but Theodora, armoured in her own thoughts and fears, did not hear more than the words themselves.

"Once, when I was a child," she said carefully, unaware of the smile of one to whom she would always be that, "I asked you about my father. And that time you told me I was too young to understand, and that when I was grown, and a woman, you would tell me."

The soft, quietly uttered words shattered the calm of the room like a handful of stones thrown to mar the smooth surface of a pond. There was a small, charged silence. Then Theodora raised her head for the first time and looked at Mrs. Allendale.

The older woman met that candid, beseeching gaze and knew that this moment she had dreaded for years could not, this time, be evaded. Knowing her child as she did, raising her along from infancy, so that all her life they had been all in all to one another, companion, friend, and

family in one, she knew that she had only to show the
smallest hint of unwillingness, and the awkward question
would be withdrawn without rancour. She knew also,
however, that to deny her now would be to flaw the almost perfect openness and trust that had hitherto existed
between them. It would still be there, but marred, as one
incautious footprint spoiled the immaculate cover of new-
fallen snow that could never be smoothed back again.

Mrs. Allendale placed the almost completed manu-
script into a cardboard folder, lovingly made and decorated by Theodora's childish hands years before, and tied
the tapes to show that she was finishing for the day. Closing the small desk on its table-top, she rose, and moved to
an armchair by the fire, inviting her daughter with a gesture to come closer. Theodora laid down her sewing and
came, her feet in their small kid shoes soundless on the thin
carpet, to sit on her accustomed low stool at her mother's
side. She leaned confidingly on her mother's knee, resting
her cheek on one hand and reaching the other up to clasp
the older one, as always slightly ink-stained, that was held
down to her.

They sat, the one waiting, the other searching mind and
heart for the right words. Mrs. Allendale looked fondly
round the room, thinking how many times they had sat so,
and wondering how often, in the future, they would sit
again. As always, the room soothed and cheered her. The
cottage might be small, even poor to some, but in here she
had allowed herself the luxury of a place that suited her
birth and her upbringing. Two rooms had been knocked
into one, and tall sash windows, two of them, had been put
in, allowing the sunlight to flood in. The carpet, though
old and worn, was Aubusson, its soft colours of rose and
azure echoed in the chintz curtains, and in the upholstery
of the set of rosewood chairs. They, with the small piano,
tables, and bookcases, she had bought all those years ago.

They had been new then, in the antique style, and they were still fashionable, eschewing as they did the over-elaboration of the Egyptian style made fashionable since Napoleon's Egyptian campaign, and seized on with such enthusiasm by the Prince of Wales. Or rather, as she supposed she must learn to call him, the Prince Regent.

Theodora waited, her mingled excitement and anxiety betrayed only in the slight flush that still coloured her cheeks, and in a little tremble apparent to her mother in their clasped hands. Mrs. Allendale gave the tremulous hand a reassuring squeeze.

"You know I was just your age when you were born?" she began. A small dimpling smile lit the face that turned up to her.

"I do, Mama, for, knowing that you were thirty-six at your last birthday, my great mathematical brain enabled me to work it out!" They shared a smile. As her daughter's only teacher and instructor, Mrs. Allendale was only too well aware that the "great mathematical brain" was sadly lacking in skill. Her smile faded as she tried to put herself into her daughter's place, and failed. How could she make this cherished child understand her own childhood? The only similarity was that it had been equally sheltered, equally cut off from the world. But the reasons for that could not have been more different. Theodora was looking up at her, with trust and apprehension mingled in her face. Mrs. Allendale drew a deep breath, and embarked on her explanation.

Orphaned at an early age, she had been left in the care of her uncle, her father's stepbrother. Wealthy himself, he had not been so dishonest as to show any interest in the modest fortune left her by her own parents. Cold and ambitious, he had educated her with a view to her making a good match, preferably with a man who would be in a position to advance his own political ambitions. To this end

he had chosen a governess both plain and elderly, who
would not complain at the secluded life she must lead, but
he had chosen better than he knew, for Miss Roxby had
given her young charge the only affection and security that
she was to know. He himself visited but rarely, and, though
his niece feared and dreaded him, she was not often
obliged to undergo the misery of his visits. The death of
Miss Roxby had marked a turning point in this quiet existence.

"I was just past sixteen, and I was desolate. My only
hope was that now, soon, I might be allowed out into the
world. Why else, I reasoned, should my uncle have been so
insistent on my being proficient in the feminine arts and
accomplishments? Like most young girls, I dreamed of
parties, and dancing, of young men and one day, a husband." She glanced at Theodora, who nodded a shy ac-
knowledgement.

"No need for those conscious looks, Dora! It is right
that a young girl should dream a little of the future. My
uncle, though, had other plans for me."

She paused, absently stroking the hand she held.

"Your skin is rough. Did you not say that Mag had
given you something for your hands?"

"Yes. I will put some on tonight. Oh, please go on,
Mama. What did your uncle want of you? Did he take all
your money? I know we are not well off, and that if you
did not sell your stories we should be quite poor."

Mrs. Allendale looked amused.

"You must not be thinking he was like some wicked
uncle in a fairy tale! He was hard and unfeeling, it is true,
but he was scrupulously honest, as my poor father must
have known when he made me his ward. He would have
scorned to touch a penny that was mine."

The young woman had assumed that she would now be
taken out into the world but her uncle, having raised her

to his own ends, had no intention of allowing her such licence. Instead, he engaged an elderly chaperon, and took to visiting more frequently, always accompanied by some other man. One of them, Sir George Waverton, became a regular visitor, but in her innocence Theodora's mother had regarded him in the light of another uncle, and submitted to his occasional kisses and fondlings without giving a thought to their cause.

"Then, one day, my uncle came to me and told me he had good news for me. I, thinking the date had been set for me to come out, was all pleasure. Then he told me I had been lucky enough to capture the interest of this man, Sir George Waverton. He had been kind enough to offer me marriage, and my uncle informed me that he himself had given his acceptance, and that I might consider myself betrothed."

Theodora's eyes filled with sympathetic tears.

"Do not be distressed, darling. It is all so long ago, so far away. I can speak of it as a story happening to someone else. I am sorry to make so long a tale out of it, but I want you to understand what happened, and why. That is very important."

"Do you really not mind speaking of it?"

"Really not. Oh, at the time I was angry, and frightened. I begged, I refused, I protested that I did not—I could not—love him. My uncle told me that such emotions were not for us. Only the lower orders might choose according to the dictates of the heart. To him, I believe, love was no more than an animal instinct, allowable in the vulgar but to be suppressed in people of breeding. "Marriage, for us," he told me, "is a matter of diplomacy, of arrangement." He even congratulated himself on his goodness in allowing me to get to know my future master, and taxed me to tell him if I did not like him well enough. I answered, in truth, that I liked him well as a friend or another uncle, but that I could not think of tying myself to him as a husband.

"At that my uncle was very angry, more than I had ever seen him before. He accused me of ingratitude—after his care of me and of my fortune—of disobedience and wilfulness. He told me that I had, at rising seventeen, four more years before I was out of his care, and that my fortune was under his control until I should marry to his satisfaction, and after his death in the hands of any lawyer he should nominate. If I was so self-willed as to continue in my obstinate refusal, then I would stay in that house, seeing no one but my uncle, and if at twenty-one I chose to leave it, it would be as a pauper. Under such duress, what was I to do? I have wondered, since, what would have happened if I had held to my decision, whether he would really have kept me so, a virtual prisoner. As it was, I wept, and pleaded, and at length gave in and agreed. At the very least, I thought, it would be a chance to go into the world a little."

But it was not to be. Sir George had no intention of taking his pretty young wife among the temptations and pleasures of Society, and kept her as closely confined as she had ever been before. After a while this quiet existence palled, and he would disappear for days or weeks. His wife soon learned the reason for these absences—he was a gambler. Though she did not know it, her own fortune was dwindling at each turn of the card, each throw of the dice, and soon her husband was taking refuge from her reproachful looks, and his own conscience, in drink. When the day came that, for fear of his drunken rage, she locked herself into her room, only to have the door broken down and herself badly beaten, she resolved to run away. Taking the only things of value she possessed—her mother's jewels—she had fled, and ended up in East Grinstead, the furthest she could go using the small amount of money in her purse, where she fell ill.

The landlady, taking pity on her youth and obvious gentility, had called a doctor.

"That dear, kind old man! You will not remember him, but no words can describe his goodness to me. In my weakness I told him my story, and he took me into his own house, and he and his wife cared for me as tenderly as if I had been their own daughter."

For the first time Mrs. Allendale had to stop, her voice suspended by emotion. Theodora stroked her inky hand, and presently her mother wiped her eyes, and smiled.

"I don't know why it is that I can tell you the saddest parts of my story without a twinge, but the minute I remember that act of kindness I am quite overset! It is a happy memory, however, and my story is nearly told.

"I was ill for several days, very ill. They nursed me, and when I was stronger he told me what I should have known for myself—that I was expecting a child. Brought up as I had been, by my dear governess, and with no married woman to talk to me or teach me, I had no idea of such things. Then I was doubly terrified—that my illness should have harmed my baby, and, worse, that Sir George might take the child from me."

"Oh, surely not! No one could be so cruel! It would not be allowed, would it?"

"Not immediately, perhaps, but after a time. A father has complete rights over his children, my dear, and yours had done nothing he was not entitled, by law, to do. By running away from him I had forfeited the protection of the law, and if he had chosen, he might have taken steps to have his child back.

"Dr. Tantobie undertook to communicate with my husband, by letter and under another name, keeping my whereabouts a secret. He received no answer. In the end he travelled to him, and found him almost stupefied with drink. When at last he understood what the doctor was saying, he replied that I might go where I willed, but I should have nothing from him. Indeed, there was precious little to have, for my fortune was gone. As for my child, if it should be a boy, he would exert every pressure of the law to have him from me, but if it were a girl I might have it and welcome, as he had no use for it. He would say no more, and almost threw the old man from the house.''

Dr. Tantobie had also written to her uncle, pointing out the scandal that would be caused if it were known that his only relative was living, destitute, on the charity of strangers. His response had been to offer a small allowance, on the condition that his niece never communicated with him again, or used her maiden or her married name.

''You may imagine, I think, how I prayed for a daughter during the months that followed, and how I rejoiced when you were born! That is why I chose your name, 'Gift of God,' for I felt you were indeed that. If I had borne a son, I had resolved that I must return with him to Sir George, and beg him to let me stay. As it was I was free— free to stay here, and make a home for us both. There is my story, then. I hope you can understand it, and forgive me— not only that I have kept you out of your rightful sphere of life, but also that I have waited so long to tell you the truth. I was afraid, you see, that you would hate me.''

Theodora rose to her knees so that she might embrace her mother.

''Forgive? Hate you? How can there be anything for me to forgive, when you have given me so much? As for hating you...I could only be cross with you for thinking such a thing! I am so sorry for you, and so glad you ran away as you did! How brave you were! I am so happy you have told me, at last.''

"Perhaps I should have told you sooner. I hesitated, also, because I did not want you to think too badly of your father. You are old enough now, I hope, to understand a little. He was not a bad man. His greatest fault was in marrying one so young, so inexperienced. It is true that he both drank and gambled, but so does many another. I would have you think of him as unfortunate, led by friends who were both richer and stronger-headed than he was."

"He did not want me," pointed out Theodora in a small, sad voice.

"My dearest, he never knew you. It is true that he wanted you less than I did, but that is true of most men, I think. He never saw you, never held you in his arms, or he might have felt differently. And he did not forget you. Though by his own standards he died a poor man, yet such fortune as was not entailed was left to you."

"When did he die?"

"In 1798, when you were four. I was not sent for, though I would have gone to him, but his end came very suddenly. There was almost no warning. I believe he had a fall on the hunting field, and died very shortly afterwards."

"You were but twenty-two yourself then, Mama. You could have married again."

"Maybe so. But a penniless widow, with a small child, is no great catch, my love! I had no wish to tie myself to another loveless marriage."

"There was my money—you could have had that!"

Her mother laughed.

"How like you to say such a thing—generous, and completely impractical! Your father's lawyers would have had a thing or two to say about that, and, in any case, I would not have done it even if it had been possible. I am very content with my life here. I have always lived a solitary kind of existence, and I have grown into a solitary kind of woman, I fear. I do not long any more for the life of London and Society. Indeed, on my few visits to that city I have found the noise and bustle almost more than I can bear. Here I have my few good friends, I can be busy and useful, and you know I am never lonely when I have a story to write.''

''You do not need to be lonely, anyway. You have me.''

''But not forever, dearest one. Do not suppose that because I am satisfied with such a life, I expect you to live it also.''

''But I am happy here with you, Mama. Do not send me away!'' Theodora clung to her mother.

''I do not mean to send you anywhere you do not want to go, foolish child. But as you pointed out, Theodora, you are a woman now, and it is time you saw a bit of the world. Why else do you think I have been so careful to have subscriptions to newspapers and periodicals, and to obtain the latest books and music? You should see Society, and be seen also. My whole aim is to prevent you from falling into a marriage such as mine. You have birth, youth, and beauty—do not shake your head—and a few thousand pounds as well, so you may hold up your head in any company.''

''But how is it to be managed? Will you take me to London?''

''I? No. I cannot present you to the polite world, for I have no acquaintance there. I do intend that you shall go up for the season, though, this very year, if it can be managed. I have written to your trustees for their advice and help in the matter. I cannot say they have been very encouraging, so far, but I am determined, and you may be sure I will find a way.''

''Oh, Mama!'' Dazzling visions of balls, soirées, theatres, and all the haunts of fashion floated before

Theodora's enchanted gaze, banishing all other thoughts from her head.

"Of course, we must be sensible. Almack's we may not hope for, I fear. As to a Presentation, I do not know. You need someone to sponsor you. Of course, what the arrangements will be, with the poor King permanently mad, and the Prince of Wales as Regent, I do not know."

Theodora came back to earth. "Mama, what shall I be called?"

"Why, by your name, of course. Theodora Waverton."

"What about your uncle?"

"I do not feel myself bound any more. Once I was able to support us by my writing, I ceased to accept his allowance. Besides, it is all so long ago, and your father is dead these fourteen years. No one will be likely to remember anything about it."

"It will be difficult to get used to it. I shall have to remember to answer. Oh, Mama, I have just thought! You are Lady Waverton!"

"Of course I am, foolish one! Does it make any difference?"

"I suppose not, and yet... I don't know, somehow it does. Is that dreadful of me? 'My mother, Lady Waverton!'"

Theodora found her head spinning. She had, at first, thought that the happiest moment was in learning that she was not a nameless, fatherless child but the daughter of a baronet, however dissolute. To find that she was actually to become a part of that world was almost more than she could take in.

"Something will turn up, I am sure of it, Mama!" she exclaimed with blithe optimism.

"Yes, I do believe it will." Her mother, for once, was caught up in Theodora's enthusiasm. "I only wish I knew what, and when," she added, more cautiously.

Looking back at her fears of the previous night, Theodora blushed at the memory of her doubts. How could she ever have considered, even for one moment, that her mother could have acted so wrongly? As to her own feelings, she resolved to put from her mind the memory of that kiss, and if that handsome face continued to intrude before her mind's eye she would banish it forthwith.

Unknown to her, the owner of that face was thinking much the same thoughts. His errand had proved fruitless; he had not found the one he had come to seek, nor even any trace of him. His embarrassed host, feeling that he had not exercised as much care as he might have done, sought to distract him with company, and had invited his neighbours to dine, with particular emphasis on those with newly adult daughters. His distinguished guest cast a disgruntled eye over the bevy of hopefuls, blushing, giggling and chattering, and thought sourly that none of them could hold a candle to his chance-met beauty. Nothing that fine gowns and careful hairdressing and hothouse flowers could do would give these girls anything more than well-bred insipidity. He allowed the idea of kissing them to cross his mind, and wondered how they would react. Not with such swift retaliation, he was bound! Nor, he realised, was he tempted in the slightest to behave with such impropriety.

"I don't know what's got into me," he muttered to himself. "All this irritation must be addling my brain! Kissing strange girls, forsooth, and admiring them for kicking me on the shins." His lips curved into a smile as he remembered his valet's shocked expression at the marks on his cherished top-boots, and his even more horrified look at the bruises, now colouring well to an interesting shade of purple, that decorated his leg.

Her face, shadowed in the dusk by the hood of her cloak, had retained its beauty in his memory, and he found himself thinking more often than was agreeable of the way her lips had responded to his kiss. A hussy, perhaps? He thought not. An innocent, then, unaware of her own attractions and unused to the presence of men. If he had thought to ask her name...

He gave himself a brisk shake, and once again put her from his mind. His host, he realised, was looking at him in anxious surprise, and had obviously been speaking to him. He recalled his scattered wits, and exerted himself to be a comfortable guest.

CHAPTER THREE

IN THE MIDDLE of the day, Theodora and her mother were accustomed to partake of a light luncheon, usually soup, bread, and fruit, with perhaps some cold meats for Theodora, who had a healthy appetite. This day, hungrier than usual, since apprehension had spoiled her breakfast, Theodora made good inroads on a cold pie, left from the previous evening, as well as some soup and no less than three apples, rather wizened from storing but still juicy and sweet. She also contrived to chatter almost without ceasing.

Mrs. Allendale, or, as Theodora called her in every other breath, Lady Waverton, found herself suffering from a headache, brought on by the tensions and emotions of the morning, and suggested mildly that her daughter might like to use up some of her superabundant energy by taking a healthy walk, since the weather continued fine.

"Yes, I will," agreed Theodora cordially. "And you shall have a lovely, peaceful afternoon to finish writing your story, *best* of mothers!"

Lady Waverton smiled her assent, promising herself privately that she would spend the lovely, peaceful afternoon on her day-bed, with her eyes closed. Nothing, she knew, would be worse than to admit her discomfort, for that would bring Theodora, all solicitude and bouncing affection, to forsake her walk and spend her time making her mother's couch hideous with offers to read aloud, fetch her unnecessary drinks, or bathe her brow with lavender-water. It was therefore with relief that she waved a fond goodbye to her daughter, noting absently that her cloak was really too old to wear for anything other than gardening, and that she had taken the dog with her, which undoubtedly meant trouble in the future.

It was not until she came to put on her cloak that Theodora thought of taking the dog. The excitements of the morning had put yesterday's events quite out of her head until she saw once again that annoying triangular tear where the thorns had caught. Now, putting on her sturdy boots and buttoning her gloves, she remembered the man she had met. It was not likely, of course, that he would cross her path again. The Forest was huge, and they were miles from whatever great house he might be staying in. Besides, she was warned now. Knowing the Forest as she did, it would be easy to hide should she hear him coming.

Nevertheless, she went to the back of the house and fetched Jason. This animal, of indeterminate and probably involved ancestry, was a large brindled beast, found when a small puppy by Theodora as he was being tormented by some boys. Never one to be daunted by superior size or numbers, she had flung herself enthusiastically into the fray. Her energy, aided probably by the sound of her educated speech which, to the boys, meant authority and trouble, had carried the day, and she had come home with a splendid black eye, and the puppy.

"I couldn't have left him there," she had pointed out. "Those horrid boys would have come back and been worse than ever, and he would have died."

Her mother had eyed the bedraggled object, noting its extremely large feet and the coat which even under the mud was thick and heavy, presaging an ability to carry quantities of dirt into any establishment.

"His name's Jason," her daughter informed her. "Look, his fur's all golden." It was, in places.

"But darling, we don't even know whether it is a male dog," she prevaricated.

"I do. I looked." Theodora was nothing if not direct. "Besides, we ought to have a guard dog. Three chickens went the other month, remember, and you said so then."

Lady Waverton had bowed with a good grace to the inevitable. As she had expected, the puppy had a voracious appetite, with a rate of growth to match. He also had a nature so friendly that it was positively embarrassing. No living creature passed him by without a wide-spreading swish of his feathered tail, strong enough to knock over small items of furniture and, if he could reach them, a bounding leap to bestow, as generously as possible, an enthusiastic licking. This display was accompanied by a volley of barks, frequently misinterpreted by strangers, so that he made, as Theodora had predicted, an excellent, if unreliable, guard dog. Theodora said that he had a sweet and loving nature, to be unaffected by his early trials. Most other people thought he was a little lacking in his wits.

The main problem with Jason was that he loved *all* his fellow creatures, not just people. Nothing was safe from his happy affection. Horses, chickens, geese, pheasants—all, he seemed to think, put on to the earth as playmates. The fact that most of them ran away from his exuberant welcome was merely, he thought, an invitation to a game. It was not that he had ever actually harmed the creatures, if he caught them. Those that died, died of fright. This, however, did nothing to make him more acceptable to the hen-wives, riders, or gamekeepers, who began to arrive in a steady stream to complain about the dog's behaviour. As Jason appeared to be completely impervious to reason, threats, or attempts to train him, he was therefore confined, and might only take his exercise under strict supervision. In sheep-keeping country it would have been impossible, but in the Forest he was—just—safe.

Theodora was his goddess and, as far as it was in him to be obedient, he was obedient to her. She, therefore, was accustomed to taking him with her when she walked out. No one had ever troubled her on her solitary rambles, possibly because, whatever his failings, his large size and loud bark made him look fierce. Lady Waverton could only hope that, should some mishap ever occur, Jason would be moved to protect his young mistress, and not indulge in a playful romp with her attacker.

The path Theodora took was a familiar one. In the bright light of day everything looked very different from the evening when she had encountered that dreadful man, and there was little to bring him to her mind. He was certainly far away by now, she thought with a little pang that annoyed her more than anything. Surely, after the way he had behaved, she was not regretting that she would never see him again? Sternly repressing the thought that he was certainly very handsome, and even rather romantic, she brought her mind back to the real world, and the story her mother had told her.

Since he had not had a long walk for at least two days, Jason was in ecstasy to be allowed out, galloping in circles and returning every few minutes to bounce round Theodora, who, with several years of experience, now automatically made sure that she had a tree to hold on to or to lean against when he threw himself lovingly at her, grinning, his tongue hanging like a loop of wet pink velvet between an alarming set of teeth. This was all so much in the usual pattern of their walks that Theodora wasted no thought on the dog, but lost herself instead in a reverie. She found it hard to believe that she would ever really go to London and enjoy all the delights of coming out, but nevertheless it was a very satisfactory daydream. So involved was she in planning rich and wonderful gowns for herself that once again she quite failed to hear the approach of hoofbeats.

As before he was riding fast, and was forced to pull up quickly, as she was in the middle of the broad track, floating happily along in a daze of silk, organza, tiffany and tulle. Jason, to whom the sight of the horse would have been almost unbearably exciting, was fortunately near enough for Theodora to make a grab for his collar. It took all her strength to keep him under control, and for a few moments she wrestled with him. His joyful barking made any speech impossible, and she was unable to look up, but the view she had from the corner of her eye was unnervingly familiar, and she found her cheeks growing pink.

At last Jason, having nearly strangled himself trying to pull away, consented to stand wheezing and panting, and she nerved herself to look up. He smiled that alarming smile that she remembered only too well.

"Another dragon, Phoebe?"

"Not at all," she said crossly, quite forgetting to disguise her speech. "I wish you would ride on, sir. You are upsetting my dog."

"Oh, is that what you call it? A local breed, no doubt?" He ran his eyes over her. Since her gown was of muslin, she had put on a blue pelisse as well as her old cloak, with a bonnet trimmed with ribbon of the same colours. Why she had chosen this, one of her more becoming garments, she did not pause to ask herself, for she could scarcely have expected to meet her tormenter again, could she? It was a simple outfit, plainly made as befitted her age, but of good quality and well fitting. No hand-me-down, he thought. He lifted one eyebrow.

"Now, what are you about today? Collecting firewood, perhaps, for your aged mother to burn in your hovel? Or gathering berries for your supper?"

"In February?" she said crossly. "We should go very hungry, I fear."

"Then you are not the poor but honest daughter of some local woodsman? Now, what can have made me think that you were?"

She bit her lip and frowned, fighting back the urge to laugh.

"If you were not convinced by my pretence yesterday, I wonder that you behaved in so ungentlemanly a way."

"Shocking, wasn't it?" he said cheerfully. "Are you sure you don't need help with that dragon?"

Theodora lost any inclination to smile.

"Certainly not. And I should warn you that he is very fierce. If I were to release him, I would not like to answer for the consequences!"

"Just as well, for I am busy this morning," was his maddeningly calm reply. "I will wish you a good day, then." She was even prettier in the full light of day than he had thought—the sunlight glinted auburn lights in her chestnut hair, and the blue of her pelisse made her eyes, in contrast, less blue than deep violet. He wondered whether his behaviour had been a mistake; it was not often that one encountered such beauty and such spirit as well. She was obviously well-born, and had he met her in London he might have enjoyed a flirtation with her. If only he had not to concern himself over this confounded business...

In the contrary fashion of a young girl, Theodora found herself disappointed when he took her dismissal so easily, and rode off. Not, of course, that she would want him to repeat his truly shocking behaviour of the night before...but there was no denying that he was very handsome, and with a decided air of fashion. If—when—she went to London, she might see him again...

She had covered about a mile and, lost in a reverie, Theodora had not noticed that it was some time since she had seen Jason. When she heard a flurry of excited barks, issuing from a thicket, she was not much alarmed, merely calling the dog to her. The barking continued, and he did not come. Irritated, she gave the special whistle which usually brought him running. He was, she supposed, attempting to form an abiding friendship with some foolhardy rabbit, or pheasant, though to be sure the weather was still very cold, and the rabbits, at least, would be safely underground at this hour. She quickened her pace, hoping it was not a pheasant.

Plunging into the thicket, the dog's bark now so loud that nothing else was distinguishable, Theodora made as much speed as she could, hoping that her cloak would not be torn beyond repair, or that it would, at least, protect her gown from the undergrowth. At last, forcing her way through a tangle of hazel where coppicing had left a stand of short stools, each one sprouting a crown of new growth, she came to a small open space, and stopped in amazement.

Lying on the ground at her feet, Jason bouncing and barking with hysterical pleasure round him, was a young man. His clothes were muddy and torn, but nothing could hide the excellence of their cut and fabric, while his shirt and neckcloth, though regrettably marked by Jason's loving attentions, had been snowy-white not long since. His hair, rather long, was tumbled in strands of corn gold against the leafy ground . . . and his face!

Theodora drew her breath in a gasp, conscious of a feeling akin to awe. The skin almost as white as marble, the finely drawn planes could have served as the model for some statue from the ancient world—Paris, say, or Apollo. She thought, in some confusion, that she had never seen such beauty in a male face. His eyes opened, and looked up at her with a gaze as blue as her own.

His lips moved, but she could not hear his voice. Jason, delighted to have his new friend in so accessible a position, crouched down to give him what he obviously felt was a much needed wash, his tail stirring up a positive blizzard of fallen leaves. The young man threw up an arm to protect his face, and Theodora saw that one leg was twisted at an awkward angle. With an exclamation of distress she darted forward, and seized Jason by his collar, exerting her full strength to haul him away so that his barks took on a wheezy, throttled tone.

"Oh, dear... I'm so sorry... he's just friendly, you know—be *quiet*, Jason—he doesn't mean any harm—Jason! Stop pulling! Are you hurt?"

He smiled, but she saw him wince as he tried to move.

"It's my leg. I fell ..."

"Oh, don't try to move! It might do more harm. Is it very bad?"

"I can move the toes on both my feet, so I have not injured anything else, I hope. I had a crack on the head, though." He paused for breath, alarmingly pale. "I must have passed out for a while, I think, and I woke up just as your dog found me."

"I'm so sorry, I'm afraid he's rather friendly—stop *pulling*, Jason!—I hope he didn't hurt you?"

"No, but I was alarmed for a minute! I couldn't think what he was. I think I addled my brains a little; I thought he was a lion, just for a moment!"

"Yes, that ruff of hair does look like a mane, I always think. The trouble is, I dare not let go of him to help you."

"I'm afraid I do not think I could stand. I did try, once, but it was rather bad. That's when I passed out."

"I must go for help, but I hate to leave you like this!" Fingers trembling from cold and excitement, she fumbled in the large pocket with which her cloak was fortunately supplied, and withdrew a length of cord, which she managed to use to fasten the dog, now almost hoarse, to a stout piece of hazel. "You will certainly catch pneumonia if you lie too long on that damp ground." She unfastened her cloak and, ignoring his protests, tucked it warmly round him, lifting his head so that she might tuck the hood underneath it. "I shan't be cold—I shall be running. It won't be long, I promise. Shall I leave Jason, for company?"

"No, thank you." His eyes regarded her earnestly. "The thing is, I do not want anyone else to find me."

"But you cannot stay here!"

"No, of course not. It is difficult to explain, but I have reasons . . . I think I may be followed. I do not want him to find me."

"Who?" Theodora never let any feeling of modesty inhibit her on her quest for information. His eyes glanced round, as if he feared there might be listening ears in the undergrowth.

"My guardian. I think . . . I am afraid . . . he wishes me ill."

"How dreadful! He must be a very wicked man!"

He shuddered.

"If you knew the whole—"

"Well, I hope you will tell me, but now I must fetch help! Keep very quiet, and I am sure no one will find you here. I will be back as quickly as I can."

He gave a faint smile, and closed his eyes. With one last worried glance, Theodora untied the cord from the tree and struggled back through the bushes, dragging a reluctant Jason. Once she reached a path, however, and started to run, he joined in happily, easily keeping pace with her, and she was forced to shorten the cord to prevent his circling her and tying her up. In a commendably short space of time, she arrived, panting, at the house. Lady Waverton, aroused by the commotion of her arrival, abandoned her rest and came to the top of the stairs.

"What is the matter, Dora? Is something wrong?"

Her daughter looked up at her, face pink and damp, chest heaving, and eyes sparking with excitement.

"I've found a man," she announced. "A young man. In the woods. He's hurt."

"Dear me," said her mother calmly. "What sort of young man, and how badly hurt?"

"Very nice," said Theodora uninformatively. "It's his leg. It might be broken, I think. And he doesn't want to be found."

"Poaching? It's not a mantrap, is it, Dora?"

"Oh, no, not that sort of young man! He's a gentleman, and he's had a fall from his horse, and he doesn't want his guardian to find him!" Theodora was regaining her breath. "We must fetch him, Mama! He's been lying on the ground, in the cold, and he could die!"

"Well, we must certainly do something. How far away is he?" Her headache forgotten, Lady Waverton acted with speed, organising the gardener and their only manservant, who combined the office of butler, footman, and general factotum in his taciturn person. A hurdle was fetched and swiftly padded with blankets, and Theodora donned her mother's cloak. Rather against her will, her mother was compelled to let her go with the men, as she was the only one able to tell them where the young man was.

He lay as she had left him, his eyes anxiously searching as he heard the sound of their approach.

"It's all right, it's me," she called, with her accustomed disregard for the finer points of the niceties of grammar. He achieved a weak smile, but she was not surprised when, being moved on to the improvised stretcher, he gave a little moan, and fainted. It gave them a chance to cut off his boot, and ascertain that the leg was indeed broken.

"The cold is worse than the hurt, miss," said the man-servant. "How long's he been lying here?"

"I don't know. We must get him back as quickly as possible. At least, if he has fainted, we might hurry more."

They arrived back to find that Lady Waverton had already summoned the doctor.

"You may take him upstairs, Whitrigg, and get him into bed. There is a fire lit in the blue chamber, and the bed is warmed." She moved to one side to allow the hurdle to manoeuvre through the door. They had wrapped him in a blanket, but it had fallen back to reveal the tousled gold of his hair, and she laid her hand on his forehead, smoothing the locks back. His eyes opened. Lady Waverton, perceiving for the first time the classic beauty of his face, blinked a little, and cast a slightly worried glance at her daughter.

"I'm sorry," he said, his husky voice and shy manner revealing his youth. "I am causing so much trouble. I did not mean them to bring me here..."

She gave him a kindly smile.

"I told them to bring you," she said comfortably. "You cannot lie out in the cold, and there is no need to worry. You are not causing any trouble."

"I can repay you," he said. "That is... not at the moment, but soon..." He foundered, crimson, and she hid her smile.

"Of course you may, if you want, but there is no need to worry about that now. If you will feel more comfortable, I shall keep account of the doctor's bills, and any other expenses. I expect you are out of funds, until the next quarter?"

He nodded, relieved, but his eyes still anxiously fixed on hers.

"It sounds strange, I know, but would you mind not telling anyone that I am here? I have a very particular reason for asking."

"My dear boy, there is nobody to tell!" she answered in some exasperation. "We are miles from the nearest village, even. As for the doctor, you will have to ask him for yourself. I cannot have it appear that I am hiding a fugitive in my house! You may rest assured, however, that I am more than equal to dealing with any dangers, real or imaginary, you might apprehend. Now let them take you upstairs, and Whitrigg will help you into bed. The doctor will be here shortly."

Indeed, almost as she spoke, a clatter of hoofs and a bustle outside proclaimed that he was already there. Theodora, who knew him well, flew to open the door to him. He received her flood of explanation, welcome, and speculation, turning to her mother with a twinkle in his eyes.

"Still the same gabble-monger, I see! First she brings home puppies, and fledgling birds that have fallen from their nests, and now it is a young man with an injured leg. Whatever will she find next, I wonder?"

"I hate to imagine," replied Lady Waverton, with mock gloom. "Something really difficult, I expect, like a lion with a thorn in its paw, or a poor lost elephant. Whitrigg says the leg is broken, and very painful, and he has been lying on the ground for some while, I think."

"Well, let's take a look at him, then. Not you, miss! Whatever next?"

"But I found him!" protested Theodora in proprietorial tones.

"Well, I shan't run away with him. You may have him back when I've finished with him, if he's well enough."

In the event the doctor professed himself moderately satisfied with the young man's condition. The break was a clean one, and soon set, though the pain of it tried the young man's fortitude not a little. The stranger was slightly feverish, but the doctor was sanguine that, by putting him straight in a warmed bed, with hot bricks to his feet and a plentiful supply of warm drinks, the danger of serious harm would be averted.

"Are you subject to colds and problems with your chest, in general?" he asked, taking the young man's pulse and noting, without appearing to, the white slender hands and the pale, fine-drawn face, which flushed a little.

"As a child, I was. But I have grown out of it now, I believe. Just because I am not out on a horse, day and night, or spending half my time shooting things, does not mean I have no strength."

"Of course it does not. You will have to keep your weight off that leg for some while, but, though it might not feel like it now, there is nothing that will not mend. It will be painful, for a while. I will leave something with Mrs. Allendale that will help you to sleep for a night or two. And your name, young man?" The question was slipped in so naturally that the patient, drowsy in any case with the warmth of the room and the aftermath of pain, started to answer without thinking.

"Edmund L—er—Edmund Lane," he stammered. "Doctor, I should be glad if . . . if you would not mention to anyone that you have seen me."

The doctor raised an eyebrow.

"Surely you will want to inform your friends of your whereabouts? Will your family not be worried about you?"

"Oh, no, they will not be expecting to see me for some while." He looked anxiously at the older man, and at Lady Waverton, who continued to regard him steadily. The doctor raised an eyebrow.

"You've not run away from school, I trust?"

"Of course not!" His disgust was genuine. "I am young, but not *that* young! It is merely that I do not want to be bullied and browbeaten! I have done nothing wrong, I give you my word!"

The doctor's severe look softened.

"Very well, Mr. Lane. I accept your reassurances. It is for Mrs. Allendale's sake, you understand. As a widow, living alone with her daughter, I cannot allow her to be imposed upon."

"Oh, no! I quite see! If my presence causes any difficulties, Mrs. Allendale, I must leave at once! I would not, for the world, cause you or Miss Allendale any distress!" He struggled to sit up, but soon subsided, white with pain.

"Lie still, and don't worry," said his hostess kindly. "No one will bully or browbeat you in this house, you may be sure, unless it is my daughter!"

"Oh, Mrs. Allendale, if I might be allowed to thank her? She saved my life, I am sure."

"Only by chance," she returned, briskly practical. "Thanks may wait for later. Now you should be sleeping, or at least resting. I will send Theodora's old nurse to sit with you." As the doctor left the room, she cast an enquiring glance at him.

"He should do well enough," he answered the look. "It is very likely that he will be feverish tonight, but your woman will know what to do. He seems to be a strong lad—the lungs are clear, and I think he cannot have been lying on the ground very long before Miss Theo found him. Well-dressed as he was, he should have taken little harm. If his condition worsens, or you have any apprehensions, do not hesitate to send for me. What do you make of him?"

"Oh, a well-brought-up boy. Inclined to exaggerate, and overreact, perhaps, as young people his age are prone to. I would say that he has, in all probability, an overbearing father, with whom he has had a disagreement. If it is true that his family will not be worried by his absence, it will do no harm to allow him to stay here for a while."

He nodded his agreement. "Yes, if you do not mind. You realised, of course, that his name is not Lane?"

She laughed. "Yes, a poor liar, and I think the better of him for it!"

To Theodora, later, she was more severe. Her daughter, frustrated in her wish to visit the patient, was voluble in her speculation about him.

"He spoke of a guardian, not a father," she reminded her mother. "He must be a very cruel man, for Mr. Lane seemed quite frightened of him! He believes he is in danger! Do you think we should set a watch tonight?"

"Who would you suggest? Cook, perhaps, relieved by the maid? We are not living in the world of romance, my dear. This is not some mysterious Gothic castle in Italy, with brigands lurking behind every rock, and sinister, murdering relatives creeping up in the dead of night to rid themselves of wealthy heirs!"

"But Mama—"

"But Mama nothing. I am quite sure he has no more to fear than a severe scolding, and for all we know he may deserve it. If he is well enough in the morning, you may sit with him for a while, with Mary, so that Nurse may get some sleep. Until then, I do not want to hear another word about him."

Their guest passed an indifferent night, and the following day the doctor was called again. He was not surprised, but said that, unless he was much mistaken, the young man was unlikely to become more ill, and should soon be on the mend. The following day he slept most of the time, and Theodora was pleased to learn, the next morning, that Mr. Lane, though rather feverish in the night, had not been worse than the doctor had predicted, and had managed to eat some breakfast. Dressing with rather more than her usual care, and wishing she had something more fashionable than her simple white muslin dresses, she availed herself of her mother's permission as soon as she was told he was awake.

Subduing her habitual ebullience, in deference to his invalid status, she entered quietly. He was sitting up against the pillows, in a very large nightshirt borrowed, she supposed, from Whitrigg, and looking alarmingly clean, which state she attributed, correctly, to the fell hand of Nurse—"Now then, Master Edmund, cleanliness is next to godliness." His corn gold hair was severely brushed, not into a fashionable disarray, but a neat schoolboy tidiness—"Come along, Master Edmund, that hair needs a good brushing."

"My goodness, you do look better!" she exclaimed. "I hope Nurse hasn't been bullying you?"

He flushed, slightly, and disclaimed, "Oh, no, she has been very kind. And I must thank you, Miss Allendale, for your good offices the other day. I do not think I did so, at the time."

"Yes, you did—three times," she informed him. "Don't worry about that now. Are you feeling better?" She gave him no time to reply, but continued headlong, pulling a chair nearer to the bed. "Actually, I should tell you that I am not Miss Allendale, but Miss Waverton. Is your guardian really an enemy to you?"

He blinked a little, unable to follow her rapid changes of subject.

"I beg your pardon, Miss Waverton, but I understood that your mother—"

"Oh, yes, she is known as Mrs. Allendale here, but she is really Lady Waverton."

"Of course, I—I understand. I should tell you, as a matter of fact, that I am not really Mr. Lane. My name is Edmund Lingdale. Um—Lord Lingdale, in fact."

"Really? How exciting! As a matter of fact, I think Mama might have guessed you gave a false name, but she is *very* understanding, I assure you. It was quite clever of you to think of it so quickly! Are you travelling incognito?"

"No! That is, yes, I suppose so." He cast an anguished glance at the maid stolidly sewing in the corner of the room.

"Oh, you need not worry about Mary! She has been with us forever! Mama said she must be here, because of the proprieties, you know. So ridiculous, when you are ill! Please tell me about your guardian! You said you were in danger from him, the other day."

He had the grace to look a little embarrassed.

"I suppose I exaggerated a bit. But he is very harsh with me, and I sometimes wonder... My father died when I was twelve, you see, and left Cousin Alexander as my guardian and trustee. I can't think why, except that his father and mine were always good friends, as well as cousins. I have not known a moment's peace since! First he was on at my mother about sending me to school, which of course she would not do, because when I was a boy I was not very strong. Now I am older he wants me to go to the university, or into the army! Not even bothering to ask me what I want to do! He is trying to force me, saying it is for my own good!"

"Into the army? But you could be killed! He sounds dreadful."

"The trouble is, my father and my grandfather were in the army, and so... but it doesn't mean that I have to! That's bad enough, but he's always telling me how to live my life. I'm always being told I should take more exercise, and learn to shoot and hunt. I don't mind riding—in fact I rather enjoy it—but I hate to see things killed. And he just can't understand!''

''No, he sounds the most brutal sort of man.''

''He is. Riding is one thing—but hunting... Only last year one of his friends was killed in an hunting accident. Yet he is always expecting me to go!''

''You don't think...?''

''I don't know,'' he said darkly. ''I know he said I was a great trouble to him, and he wished he were not burdened with me. That was when I refused to go to Leicestershire with him.''

''Why did he want you to go there?''

''Oh, I was to hunt with the Belvoir. I suppose it's meant to be an honour, or something, but I hated the idea. I should have hated it.''

''Yes, of course you would.'' With a strong effort of imagination, Theodora put herself in the place of one who would reject the chance to ride with the most fashionable hunt in the country. ''I suppose he was very angry?''

''Yes, he was. He said if I was frightened to ride with the Belvoir, I should come down to Sussex and ride with the local hunt, and he would fix up some rough shooting for me. I told him I didn't want to, and he just laughed! Said it would be good experience for me! I decided enough was enough. So the other day—the day you found me—I said I was going out for a ride, and went off! I had written to my mother, to say I meant to visit some friends, so you must not think she would have been worried.''

''How brave! Where were you going?''

''I hadn't quite decided. To London, in the end, I suppose, but I couldn't go there straight away, because they would have been sure to find me. So I travelled east, instead, and, if I had not been thrown by that curst horse, I should have been miles away by now!''

"What a shame! Never mind, we'll hide you. What became of the horse?"

"I don't know. I let go of the reins."

He looked gloomy, and she hastened to distract him.

"What do you want to do, if you don't wish to go to the university, or anything like that?"

His face lit up with enthusiasm. "I want to write!"

"To write? My mother writes stories, and articles for periodicals. Perhaps she could help you!"

"Does she?" His voice breathed awe. "I haven't done much yet, but I wrote some poems, at school, that some people thought were quite good. And the beginnings of a play, about the Young Pretender."

Theodora was impressed, and said so. Such admiration, from the most beautiful girl he had ever seen, was balm and incense to his wounded soul, and he embarked on an enthusiastic description, with such passages as he could recall, of his work. So engrossed were they, that they quite failed to hear the approach of footsteps, and it was not until the sound of a voice, just outside the door, attracted their attention that they fell silent. The door opened.

"Well, my ward, what tedious maggot has entered your brain now?" enquired the man who came in, frowning.

"You!" gasped Lord Lingdale, falling back against his pillows.

"You!" exclaimed Theodora, and fell into helpless, uncontrollable laughter.

CHAPTER FOUR

THE MAN IN THE doorway raised one dark eyebrow, and surveyed the couple before him.

"You will forgive my intrusion. I had no idea you were conducting a tête-à-tête. Should I perhaps return a little later?"

"So you are the wicked guardian! I might have known it," said Theodora, recovering her composure. Her mother followed the visitor into the room.

"Really, Theodora, I do not know when I have been so ashamed of your manners," she said crossly. "You will perceive, Mr. Ravensworth, that one of the maids is in the room. I can assure you she has been here for the entire morning."

He saw that she was ruffled, but made no attempt to apologise.

"Quite so, ma'am. Miss Allendale, I believe. And what nonsense has this young puppy been pouring into your ears?"

"It is not nonsense," she replied hotly, "and my name is not Allendale!"

"I can scarcely continue to call you Phoebe," he said with disdain. Blushing furiously, Theodora opened her mouth to reply, but was forestalled by Edmund. Crimson with mingled fury and embarrassment, he attempted an air of social ease.

"Lady Waverton, Miss Waverton, may I present to you my guardian, Mr. Alexander Ravensworth? Cousin Alexander, this is Lady Waverton, and her daughter."

"Very correct, but a trifle late, Edmund. This lady has already informed me that her name is Allendale. She also told me that the only young man in her house was called Lane. Mr. Lane. Is that correct?"

Lady Waverton did not lose her composure.

"I am, in fact, Lady Waverton, though for family reasons I prefer to be known by my mother's maiden name of Allendale, and that is the name I am called here. The reasons can be of no interest to you. As for your ward, I was aware from the start that he had given me a false name. It did not seem to me of any great importance, since he was not well enough to be moved from here."

"It did not, in fact, occur to you that he might have friends who would be worried by his absence?" His voice was icily polite, and Theodora rushed to her mother's defence.

"Of course it did. Mr. Lane—Lord Lingdale, I mean—told us that no one would be expecting him. He also told us about you, Mr. Ravensworth—enough to make us realize that you might well be pleased to be rid of him!"

To her intense irritation, the look of discomfort, or even alarm, that she had hoped to see on his face was replaced by one of amusement.

"Ah! The Wicked Guardian, I perceive!"

"Yes, and how you can smile about it, I don't know!"

"It just shows the depths of depravity to which I have fallen, my dear child."

"I am not a child, and I am certainly not your dear! In fact—"

"That will be enough, Theodora." Lady Waverton's tranquil voice broke across her daughter's. "Mr. Ravensworth, I can see no purpose in this, except that it is undoubtedly bringing on a return of your ward's fever. There can be no question of Lord Lingdale's being moved from here for some time, so I suggest that you and I go to my sitting-room, and discuss what arrangements are necessary. Theodora, I think a little quiet reflection in your room would be beneficial to us all. Perhaps you would ask Nurse, if she is awake, to come and look after our patient.''

She waited, her face calm, while Theodora battled successfully with a mutinous reply, and attempted to sweep from the room. Her dignified curtsy was returned by Mr. Ravensworth with an exquisitely urbane bow, and it was with difficulty that she refrained from slamming the door behind her. Edmund watched her go, his expression slightly hunted, then turned the eyes of a mesmerised rabbit on to his guardian, who crossed to the bedside and laid a strong, beautifully manicured hand on his forehead.

''Kindly refrain from watching me like that,'' said Mr. Ravensworth with restrained irritation. ''Have you ever known me to lay violent hands on you? Have you?''

''No, but—''

''But nothing. This ill-thought start has caused me a great deal of inconvenience, which you will not mind, and your mother a considerable amount of anxiety, which I am sure you will. If you did not wish to come down into Sussex, why did you not tell me?''

''I tried, but—'' The shameful tears were not far away. Once again Lady Waverton intervened.

''Here is Nurse, Mr. Ravensworth, with some of the medicine that the doctor left for your ward. I think he should rest now, if you will come with me?''

''You are right. This is not the time for recriminations. I will inform your mother, Edmund, that you are safe.'' He left the room without a farewell, and followed downstairs.

By the time he reached the sitting-room his temper was restored.

"I should apologise to you, Lady Waverton, for disrupting your household in this way. You have been more than kind to the boy. If you will tell me the sum of my indebtedness?"

"Of course. Our doctor is, I think, very able, but perhaps you would wish to have your own man examine him?"

"Thank you. I think his mother would like that. He is in no danger?"

"I do not think so. It was a clean break, and should heal without leaving any lasting damage. There was some fever, but it is much abated."

"Until this morning?" He acknowledged her unspoken reproof with a wry smile. "I am afraid I do not have the knack of handling the lad. He is his mother's only son, and has been very much indulged. His slight tendency to colds and coughs, as a child, has given her the fixed impression that he is delicate, and must be sheltered from every cold wind like a hothouse flower. He does not appear to be physically robust, but he has never had a serious illness in his life, and if she could only be persuaded that some time spent in the country, riding or engaging in other outdoor sports, would not harm him, he would be a great deal better off."

"A mother with an only child, Mr. Ravensworth, is inclined to cherish that child too greatly."

"Do you do so? I think not. You will pardon my blunt speaking, Lady Waverton, but you seem to be a woman of good sense, which my ward's mother is not. Lady Lingdale centres her whole existence on this young man. Everything he does is perfect. He has only to scribble two or three lines of verse, and she is puffing him off to all her acquaintance as a new Shakespeare! Now, of course, he has the idea in his head that he must be a poet, and follow his father and grandfather into the army he will not.''

''You would not wish him to enter into such a career, in these troubled times, unless he had the wish to?''

''Of course not! It was his father's greatest desire, but the army will be better without so reluctant an officer. Then I suggested the university, if he wishes to pursue a literary bent, but that was not right either! His mother has persuaded him that he has nothing to learn, and fears that the nasty rough undergraduates might teach him to drink, or game, or indulge in nameless vices!''

''Forgive me, it is not for me to interfere, but is it necessary for him to do anything at all? He is nineteen, I believe, and might be almost accounted a man.''

''You think I am too busy on his behalf? Perhaps you are right. I was only twenty-one myself when I became his guardian, and my responsibilities assumed a greater proportion than they should have done. His father might have been a great man, had he chosen, and there is much of him in his son. His fortune is respectable, but not large, and I am as anxious as his mother is that he should not waste his patrimony by getting involved in the wrong set.''

''You may relieve your mind, and hers, of that worry for a few weeks, Mr. Ravensworth. He will encounter no hard-drinking, hard-living bucks in this house.'' She looked at him quizzically.

''Except myself.'' Her slight smile acknowledged that he had correctly taken her meaning. ''It is true that I both drink, and gamble. Oh, not to be compared with Alvanley, or Brummell, but I am a member of Brooks's. The fact that I behave so does not mean I would be happy to see my ward in such surroundings.''

''Then you are protecting him also, as you blamed his mother for doing.''

"I see where Miss Waverton gets her habit of plain speaking. Lady Waverton, it can hardly have escaped your notice that your daughter and I were not strangers to one another."

She did not answer, but fixed her eyes upon him.

"You ask no questions—admirable woman! The fact is that I was down here, a few days ago, visiting the friends with whom young Edmund was to have been staying, and while out riding in the woods, I met Miss Waverton, who had had the misfortune to have her cloak tangled up in a thorn bush. I was able to help set her free."

He paused, but still she did not speak. Her silence was a rebuke. "I assume that the young lady did not mention the circumstance to you. She pretended to me—very convincingly, in fact—that she was no more than a country girl, and I kissed her."

Lady Waverton gave a faint smile.

"No wonder she did not tell me about it. And then?"

"She kicked me. Hard. And I am afraid I deserved it, for I confess I was not taken in by her charade. She did it well—very well, in fact! I exchanged a few words with her the following afternoon: Edmund had disappeared, and I was looking for him, so I was in a hurry. I am afraid I teased her."

A little frown wrinkled Lady Waverton's forehead. "She is very innocent. More so than most girls of her age, from the circumstance of our having lived so very retired. She would have no idea of the risk she ran."

"I am not in the habit of ravishing every country girl I find," he pointed out mildly.

"No, but she did not know that, did she? I think the better of you for telling me about it—trusting, of course, that the episode will not be repeated. It may have given her a useful lesson, and it certainly made her think. The following day she asked me about her father."

"Waverton? The name seems familiar."

"Sir George Waverton. I...left him, before Theodora was born."

"From what I have heard, I do not altogether blame you. I was still at school then, but he was a gambler, was he not? And that is why you live as you do?"

"Yes. As a deserting wife, I could have no place in Society. I tell you this, because it is only right that Lady Lingdale should know of the household in which her son is residing."

"You are very scrupulous. I do not think it is something that will worry her. Something else will, however. Your daughter."

Lady Waverton sighed. "I know it. But they are both so young, hardly more than children..."

"She is a very beautiful girl, and he is just the age to be forming romantic attachments. So, of course, is she."

"What can I do? To keep them apart would do more harm than good, for they would have nothing to do but think of one another. It is the greatest misfortune that she should have found him, except, of course, that the poor boy might have died if he had remained out in the cold all night."

"I would have nothing to say against such a match, for she is his equal in birth, and might well do him the world of good," Mr. Ravensworth commented.

"You make her sound like a paregoric draught," returned Lady Waverton.

"Unintentionally, you may be sure. It is his mother who might be the trouble. It has not yet occurred to her that one day she will have to lose her son to another woman."

"I think we are worrying unnecessarily over something that will probably not happen. You have not had a chance to discover that Theodora has a great deal of common sense. The best thing we can do is behave as if nothing were further from our thoughts. To separate them, or to warn them, would only put ideas into their heads. I shall keep Theodora busy, and you may be sure that they will spend no time alone together.''

Mr. Ravensworth rose.

"Once again, you put me to rights. I will take my leave of you in the hope that I may be allowed to visit again to-morrow? I must inform Edmund's mother of his where-abouts, and arrange for him to be seen by another doctor—no insult to your own man is intended, of course, but, knowing Amelia Lingdale, she will want to have her own doctor visit, at vast expense, from London."

"Will Lady Lingdale wish to visit her son? If so—"

"I shall do my best to discourage it. You have enough on your hands without entertaining strangers, and she is very exacting. Besides, I think it better if she does not set eyes on your daughter!''

Lady Waverton could not but agree with him.

Upstairs in her bedroom, Theodora had enjoyed a hearty burst of tears, and then had philosophically washed her face and sat down by the window to reflect, as her mother had suggested. Passing under review the short in-terview that had taken place, she found her hands were unconsciously clenching themselves into fists, and relaxed them. There was no doubt that she had behaved rudely, but what of him? If anyone deserved taking down a peg or two, it was Mr. Ravensworth.

The memory of his kiss seared her; with an effort she bundled the thought back into the depths of her mind, resolutely slamming the door on the recollection of her feelings. He was detestable, and a tease, and a bully too, and she would not be at all surprised if he were not plan-ning some mischief to his hapless ward.

By the time her mother came to see her, she had worked herself up into a fine crusading zeal to protect Lord Lingdale, and bring his persecutor to justice. Lady Waverton looked at the flushed, mutinous face.

"Mr. Ravensworth has gone," she said mildly.

"Good! I hope I shall never have to exchange another word with him."

"That will be difficult, since he is bound to come and visit his ward. Do you propose to spend the next few weeks up here, or would you like to go and stay with the doctor and his wife? I am sure they would have you."

"Run away from him? Certainly not!"

"Then you must try not to embarrass me by behaving as you did this afternoon. These are not the manners I have tried to teach you, my dear."

"No, Mama, and I am very sorry. But if you knew! I did not tell you before, because I did not want to vex you, but I have met Mr. Ravensworth before, when I went to visit Mag the other day."

"I know. Mr. Ravensworth confessed it."

"But I am sure he did not confess how he behaved?"

"Well, he told me he kissed you. And I have to tell you, Theodora, that you were lucky that one snatched kiss was all you received."

Her daughter hung her head.

"I'm sorry, Mama. I thought if I talked like a village girl he would leave me alone. Afterwards, I realised I had been mistaken. Oh, Mama, do all men behave so? I had thought him a gentleman."

"Not all men, darling. And he is a gentleman. He meant, I think, to teach you a lesson. I have to tell you that he was not deceived by your act, though he did say you did it very well."

"You mean . . . he knew I was a gentlewoman . . . and he still kissed me? And you say he is a gentleman?"

"Yes. And yes."

"Well, I do not. How could he?"

"As I said, to teach you a lesson. A less well-bred man, my dear, would have pretended to me that he *was* convinced by your acting, if he had ever spoken of it at all. I think you should be grateful to him."

"Grateful to him? He is the most horrible man I have ever met!"

"Then you are not likely to imagine you are forming a romantic passion for him, are you? He is very good-looking, after all," said her mother, wiser than Mr. Ravensworth in the ways of young girls.

"A romantic passion? For him? I would be as likely to fall in love with—with an adder!"

With this, Lady Waverton had to be satisfied.

Mr. Ravensworth did not, in fact, visit during the following afternoon. Theodora, who had been practising a look of dignified disdain in front of her looking-glass, and had done her hair up with more than usual care, was scornful.

"He is not even a man of his word! Did he not say he would come to see you today? Now it is nearly dark, and he will certainly not arrive."

"Thank goodness for that," replied the invalid. "I do not want to see him at all."

"No, nor do I, but if he said he would come, it is very rude of him not to," said Theodora inconsistently. "Anyway, you do not need to be afraid of him here."

"I am not afraid of him!" he responded indignantly. "I just do not want to see him! He has such a sarcastic way with him; whatever I say he seems to misunderstand me. I am sure he does it on purpose."

"Of course he does. You should not let him put you out."

"You should have heard him when I said I did not wish to go hunting with the Belvoir! And, whatever he may say, it was not because I had that fall last time he took me out hunting with him.''

"Was it bad? Were you hurt?"

"No, not really. He took a fence, and there was a ditch on the other side. I tried to follow him, because I thought he would be pleased, but I did not know about the ditch. I went over the horse's head, but the horse broke its front legs, and had to be shot.''

Theodora shivered.

"How dreadful! No wonder you did not want to go again. Was he very angry?"

"Yes. It was his horse. He was far more upset about that than about danger to me, I am sure.''

Theodora gazed at him, wide-eyed.

"You do not suppose . . . he meant you to have an accident, do you?''

Edmund looked back, all too quick to pick up her meaning.

"I do not think so," he said slowly. "He told me, at the meet, not to follow him, because I did not know the country. He said I should not risk a jump unless I was quite sure of it, and that there was no shame in going round by a gate.''

"If anyone said that to me, I would jump every hedge and fence I came to," asserted Theodora.

"Yes, and so I did," he admitted.

"Then that was what he meant you to do," she said darkly, lowering her voice so that the incurious Mary would not be likely to hear them. "It would be just like him, to tell you to do one thing so that you would do just the opposite!''

He was impressed by her reasoning, but dubious. "But he was very annoyed about the horse.''

"Of course he was! That was his mask, to cover the fact that he was *really* annoyed that you had not been killed! I expect he would have inherited your fortune, wouldn't he?''

"Yes, but—"

"There you are, then!'' She was triumphant.

"But I haven't got a fortune—not really. Oh, I don't mean I'm a pauper, or anything. There's a place in the country, and some land, and money in Funds. I suppose you could say I'm comfortably off. But Cousin Alexander is rich! Really rich, I mean. I don't really know, but I believe his income is at least forty thousand a year.''

Theodora was impressed, but was too enamoured of her theory to abandon it too easily.

"You don't think he might have gambled it all away? He told Mama he was a member of Brooks's, and they play very high there, don't they?''

"Yes, but he has the most extraordinary luck. He's known for it. And he's far too careful to bet more than he can afford. Why, he once gave me a real dressing down only for putting fifty guineas on a horse!''

"Then if it's not your fortune, it must be your title. After all, he's only a plain Mr., and you're a Lord!''

"I don't know that he cares very much for that.''

"Nonsense. Of course he does, anyone would. How cross he must have been that I found you! It would have been a lovely accident, for him, and no one could have held him responsible, for you did it all yourself!''

"You needn't remind me,'' Edmund said gloomily.

"Oh, you mustn't mind! I think you were very brave, running off like that.''

He brightened not a little.

"Now we know he will not come today, we may enjoy a comfortable evening. Would you like me to read to you, or shall we play a game?'' asked Theodora.

In the event they settled to a cheerful game of cribbage, wrangling happily over the cards like a pair of schoolchildren, all thoughts of Wicked Guardians temporarily banished.

The following morning, however, Theodora returned from exercising Jason to find a familiar horse in the yard behind the house. Putting the dog in the converted stable which served him as a home, but neglecting, in her haste, to fasten both halves of the door, she made for the house, determined to protect Edmund from danger. Such was her hurry and anxiety that she quite failed to notice Jason who, with the kind of low cunning occasionally exhibited by animals of small intelligence, was following her without barking, his feet leaving an interesting design of mud on floors and carpets, and his generous tail painting streaks of the same tint on walls, curtains and furniture. Hearing Ravensworth's voice issuing from Edmund's room, in raised tones, she flung open the door and marched in.

Jason, recognising unerringly the interesting friend who was the only human he had ever met who actually lay on the ground to be licked, gave a yelp of delight and launched himself towards the bed, his claws scratching on the polished wood floor, and his tail flailing dangerously near a small table on which reposed the various nostrums and potions that Nurse had decreed.

"Jason!" shrieked Theodora, snatching at his collar as he went by her, but foiled by a rug which, rucked by his paws, caught round her feet. "Jason, come *here!*"

Edmund, already wincing at the thought of several stone of loving, uncontrollable dog landing on top of his leg, extended hands in what the besotted animal took as a welcoming gesture. Barking a throaty welcome, he leaped for the bed, to be brought up short by Ravensworth, who caught his collar and, with one swift jerk, pulled him sideways so that the dog's paws went from under him, and he ended up on his back, still barking, but with a look of surprise that in any other circumstance would have been comical.

As it was, "Leave him alone, you brute!" shrieked Theodora.

"Don't be alarmed, Miss Waverton," Ravensworth's calm voice carried through the tumult, "He has not hurt me."

"Not him! You!" raged Theodora, letting go of the bedpost she had been forced to clutch when she tripped in coming to the help of her dog.

"My leg! Don't let him go!" moaned Edmund.

"Don't worry, I won't. Apart from other considerations, he is quite appallingly muddy," replied his guardian, keeping his grip on Jason who, having scrabbled back on to his feet, was now attempting to jump up at him to make his acquaintance, also. "Get down, sir! Down, I say!" This command, spoken sternly, caused Jason to cease his jumping, much to Theodora's mingled irritation and admiration.

"Look at that! He's stopped jumping up at you!" she exclaimed.

"It merely requires a little firmness," he told her kindly. "Do you have any other pets, or is this the only one?"

"Well, there's the kitchen cat," she began dubiously, sidetracked.

"Then kindly keep it in the kitchen. It is only a cat, I trust, and not a leopard, or a tiger?"

"Of course it is. And Jason is only a dog. He's just very... very friendly."

"So I see. Well, I am much obliged to him, but I should prefer it if he could be friendly somewhere else. I suppose he lives in your room?"

"Certainly not! He's not allowed in the house at all. I must have forgotten to bolt the door properly. I saw your horse, so naturally I was in a hurry."

"You can't imagine how flattered I am. I had no idea that my presence was so pleasing to you."

"Well, it isn't. I don't want to see you at all, and nor does Lord Lingdale."

"Then I had better go." He loosened his grip on the collar, and at once Jason made for the bed again.

Edmund cried out, "No! Not on my leg! Cousin Alexander!"

"It seems that my ward is not so averse to my presence as I thought. Can it be that he is learning to love me?" Ravensworth resumed his hold on Jason.

"Please take him away," begged Edmund to Theodora. "He is a delightful creature, and I am very grateful to him for finding me the other day, but if he should jump on my leg, I don't think I could bear it!"

"What would you have done, if I had not been here as a witness?" challenged Theodora. "Let him jump up, I suppose, and let poor Edmund's leg be hurt?"

"Well, if you had not come in, the dog would not have been here," he pointed out reasonably, "so that will have to be one of the great mysteries of the unknown. I was attempting to inform my ward, before your untimely entrance, that I went up to London yesterday, and saw his mother. I thought she would be less alarmed if I took the message myself, rather than sent a letter."

"That was kind of you," she said with grudging approval.

"Yes, wasn't it? Of course, it might be simply a blind, to cover my other evil deeds so that nobody will notice them."

"I wish you would not be so silly," Theodora said crossly, taking Jason's collar and dragging him towards the door. He whined, and set his feet, so that she had to slide him across the floor. She was bitterly aware that her skirt was muddy, and that her carefully arranged *coiffure* was slipping down her neck.

"I beg your pardon, Miss Waverton. I don't know where I get these foolish ideas from." With courtly suavity he opened the door for her, and bowed her from the room.

Edmund stiffened himself for the blast of sarcastic reproof that he expected and, he thought, probably deserved. To his surprise he received no such thing. Mr. Ravensworth seemed bent on proving himself more understanding than heretofore, and, although he naturally expressed his displeasure at his ward's behaviour, nevertheless it was not in terms that left him feeling as though all the skin had been flayed from his body, leaving him exposed to the icy air.

"Your mama, of course, has been very alarmed on your behalf, but I think I have allayed her qualms. Nevertheless, I think you should write to her frequently, and of course when you are fit to be moved you must return to London. You young cawker, if you did not wish to stay in the country, you had only to say so, you know! Now I will scold you no more, but leave you to recover in peace. Perhaps we may understand one another better, in the future."

Edmund clasped the hand held out to him, and muttered incoherent apologies and thanks.

"Yes, well, we'll say no more of that. Mind you do not make yourself a nuisance to Lady Waverton, however."

"Oh, no! I should not dream—" But his guardian was gone.

Mr. Ravensworth did not visit his ward again, but returned the following day to London. Relieved of his presence, Lord Lingdale found that his recovery proceeded apace, and soon his only complaint, apart from his worry that he was creating too much trouble in the household, was of boredom. It was in vain that Lady Waverton of-

ered him the use of her small but well-stocked library.
Company was what he craved—more specifically, the
company of her daughter.

At first it was possible to make the excuse of his health,
that too much excitement was liable to make him feverish. As the days went by, however, and his temperature
subsided, this was no longer possible. Lady Waverton attempted to keep her daughter as busy as possible with er-
rands to the village, to Mag, to anywhere which would take
her outside the house, but the short February days meant
that such outings must, of necessity, finish by four o'clock,
leaving a long evening to be filled. Unthinkable, when their
guest was languishing upstairs, to be sitting downstairs!
Lady Waverton gave in gracefully to the inevitable, and
made sure that she herself was one of the little party that
gathered every day in the guest room.

Even without her presence, their behaviour would not
have been such as to raise even the most censorious of
eyebrows. Like a pair of children, as she often called them,
they talked, read, played nursery games, squabbled, and
made up. In the mornings, when Theodora was busy, Edmund would write his poems, brow furrowed over the
portable desk that his hostess kindly lent him. They were
ponderous works, full of classical allusions and descrip-
tive imagery, and in the evening Lady Waverton's self-
command was sometimes exercised to its utmost when he
read them out. Theodora, however, was impressed, and
said so. Her mother's little stories, in everyday language
and recounting small household incidents, were very dull
by comparison. The poet, glowing with satisfaction, wrote
on, and fired by her enthusiasm embarked on a play, in
verse, about the life of Charlemagne.

"I know!" said Theodora. "We can act it out!"

"But we have not enough people, and there is no the-
atre," protested the author anxiously.

"Not really on a stage, silly! But we can try it, to see how it sounds. You know what a difference it makes when one reads things aloud. You shall take the men's parts, and I the women's. Mama shall be the audience!" Her idea was received with applause, and every evening now saw them declaiming and arguing over words, to an appreciative, if mildly hysterical, audience of one. The formalities very soon fell by the wayside—it was "Edmund" and "Theodora" in no time.

"After all, Mama, it is so cumbersome to be saying 'Lord Lingdale' and 'Miss Waverton' all the time! And we are such good friends, we might almost be brother and sister!"

Lady Waverton made no comment.

It was a heady novelty, for both of them. As single children, brought up at home by their mothers, neither of them had any experience of a friendship with young people of the same age. Theodora knew no one, boy or girl, other than the village children, with whom she had sometimes played as a child, but whom she now seldom saw, and there were nothing but polite enquiries to say on either side.

Edmund had been kept by his mother from playing with other children, on the grounds, that he might catch some ailment, or be hurt by their rough games. Of late he had made a few acquaintances—young men of birth whose position made them acceptable to his mama—but he had never done more than exchange a few words of greeting, or occasionally take part in a country dance, with a young lady. Certainly he had never encountered anyone like Theodora, who was not only beautiful, but an amusing and entertaining companion as well.

The upshot might well be imagined. With all the fervour of youth and romanticism, he decided that he was, in fact he must be, in love. His letters to his mother, written eluctantly and under a certain amount of pressure from Lady Waverton, took on a tone of eulogy, and his poems grew more sentimental and florid by the hour. Lady Lingdale took fright, and summoned her son's guardian.

CHAPTER FIVE

THE FOLLOWING MORNING, Mr. Ravensworth presented himself at Lady Lingdale's house in Mount Street, and was shown to the pretty drawing-room where his hostess, swathed in silk shawls, was reclining on a sofa.

"I do not know how you contrive to be here so quickly, Ravensworth," she complained, sitting up and straightening her turban.

"I thought you would be pleased, Cousin Amelia. Usually you say I am too slow in answering your—invitations. Naturally, I hurried round without wasting a moment."

Lady Lingdale surveyed, with a jaundiced eye, the buff pantaloons, knitted so that they fitted skin-tight to those admirable legs, the refulgent hessians and the expertly tailored dark blue coat above which his spotless linen gleamed. His neckcloth, tied in a neat Oriental, was perfection, and no haste had marred those perfect folds and creases.

"I am only surprised to find you in London," she said. "I had thought you in Sussex still."

"Nursing Edmund? I thought I had explained to you that he is being well and kindly looked after. I am not his nurse, you know."

"But to leave him there, with strangers!"

"I cannot see what good it would have done to remain there. It was made clear to me, in the politest possible way, that my presence upset the boy, and was likely to slow his recovery. You must admit that he has never been known to show any fondness for my company.''

"Is it surprising, when you are so hard on him? But I see how it is. That woman wanted you out of the way, so that she could get him into her clutches.''

"Lady Waverton? Why ever should she bother?''

"She means to entrap him with her daughter, Miss Waverton. If she is a Waverton at all, which I doubt.''

His face changed, and she shrank back against her cushions.

"It may interest you to know, Cousin Amelia, that I have pursued my own enquiries into Lady Waverton and her daughter. Not, mind you, because I thought it to be necessary, but simply because I foresaw just such a situation as this. Both Lady Waverton and her daughter are of the utmost respectability, and the girl is without doubt a daughter of Sir George, and heir to such money as he was able to leave her.''

"Well, that wouldn't be very much.''

"A few thousands. The amount is immaterial. The point is, I cannot allow you to go around maligning them. Gratitude alone should have prevented that. If it were not for the Wavertons, Edmund might well be lying in his grave by now.''

Lady Lingdale shed a few easy tears. "I know, and I am grateful to them. But Alexander, only look at this letter I had yesterday from Edmund! He is positively raving about the girl!''

"That is only to be expected. She is a very lovely girl.''

"But what am I to do?''

"Nothing at all.''

"Nothing? And let my Edmund be snapped up by a little nobody like that? How can you say such a thing?''

"Let us have this quite clear. Do you intend to keep Edmund at your side forever, and never allow him to marry?"

"Of course not! I am not quite a monster! Only he is so young, and so vulnerable."

Mr. Ravensworth, with a strong effort of will, refrained from pointing out what he had often told her before—that Edmund's vulnerability lay in his inexperience and the overprotected life he had always led.

"That is just as well. Edmund has always been an obedient son to you, but he is growing up. This latest escapade, ill-judged through it was, shows that he is no longer prepared to do everything that is arranged for him by others. If you cross him now, as he is beginning to spread his wings, you are likely to lose him altogether."

"But he is too young to marry!"

"Of course he is, and so is she. But to tell him so would be the worst move you could make. Give him his head a little, and with more experience he will soon learn it for himself."

"And if he does not?"

"If he does not, then you have no right to prevent him. Comfort yourself that you could have done far worse. The girl is well-born, well brought up, and young enough to learn to respect and obey you."

Lady Lingdale looked thoughtful, and Ravensworth, who had his own reasons for persuading her to accept Theodora, banished the memory of the headstrong, disrespectful girl he had seen not long before, and waited.

"Very well. You may be right. But I did so want him to make a good marriage. In his position, he could look for a wife of fortune, not merely with a respectable competence."

Ravensworth rose, and walked to the fireplace.

"There is one other thing I should, perhaps, tell you," he said, leaning with elegant negligence against the chimney-piece. "I told you that I have made some enquiries. You are probably not aware that Lady Waverton is the niece, or rather stepniece, of Jonas Bellerby."

"Jonas Bellerby? Good heavens, is he still alive?"

"Very much so. And, I am creditably informed, he has no other living relatives. Nor, I might add, does he have any friends."

"Well, that's not surprising. The most unpleasant man I ever met—not that I met him more than once, for he never goes anywhere. I cannot see that that is a recommendation."

"I am trying to point out to you," Ravensworth said patiently, "that Lady Waverton and her daughter are his only kin. While he has not, as far as I know, been on speaking terms with his niece for many years, he is still known to feel strongly on the subject of inheritance: that it should go wherever possible to a member of the family."

Lady Lingdale found that her mouth was hanging open, and shut it, remembering that it made her double chin more prominent.

"But he's rich as—as what's-his-name!"

"Precisely. He feathered his nest very nicely when he was working for the Government, as most of them do, and he certainly hasn't spent much of it since."

"And you think this Miss Waverton could be his heiress?"

"I cannot say anything for certain. All that I can say is that there is a likelihood. And a young lady seen to be accepted by one of the leaders of Society like yourself, my dear cousin, would make the likelihood even stronger. More than anything, Jonas Bellerby has always worshipped position."

The flattery was so unusual that Lady Lingdale let it pass without question. One was not, perhaps, a Lady Jersey, or a Princess de Lieven, but one was known, and invited, everywhere.

Ravensworth left her preening herself, not dissatisfied with his morning's work. He refrained from visiting Sussex straight away, nor did he write to his ward, who basked in the unexpected freedom from supervision and added more and more stanzas to his already unwieldy work of art.

After a week, when he judged that Edmund would be in a more rational state of mind and healthier state of body, he took himself to Sussex. Somewhere within him a little niggling devil asked him whether he would have been so prompt in his attentions had his ward not been inhabiting the same house as a very pretty girl. He treated the idea with the contempt it deserved, but there was a wry smile on his lips when he knocked at the door of Chelwood Cottage and was admitted by Whitrigg.

"How is my ward?" he enquired, handing the manservant his hat and gloves, and permitting him to remove his riding coat.

"His lordship is greatly improved, sir. Will you wait in the study while I inform Mrs.—that is, Lady Waverton?"

"No need to disturb the ladies—I came only to see the boy. Don't trouble to announce me; I know my way."

He would not admit to himself that he did not wish to give Theodora time to take herself off, but, convincing himself that he did not want to disrupt the household, strode up the stairs while Whitrigg, who was unused to visitors of so fashionable an appearance or high-handed a manner, was still uttering flustered ejaculations. Striding into the room without warning, he found Edmund and Theodora wrangling happily over a game of spillikens.

"It moved! I saw it move! Come, now, you cannot deny it!" Theodora with her back to the door, had not noticed him enter, but she caught sight of the frozen expression on Edmund's face and turned. Her own laughing look faded, replaced by one of icy displeasure. Ravensworth knew a feeling of chagrin, instantly repressed.

"Good afternoon, Edmund. I am glad to see you so much better."

"C-Cousin Alexander! Yes, thank you! Much improved!"

Theodora, her chin raised haughtily and eyes lowered in an affectation of modesty, would have left the room, but was prevented by the fact that Mr. Ravensworth was still planted solidly in the doorway. She approached, thinking that he would move, but he did not. Flustered, she drew back again.

"Ah, Miss Waverton! Good afternoon!"

She made a small, dismissing curtsy. "Mr. Ravensworth."

"Surely you will not feel yourself obliged to be driven away by my arrival? Edmund's presence, and of course that of your maid, does away with all impropriety, you know!"

"I have no fear of impropriety—now," she said, rather fiercely. "Doubtless you will wish to be private with your ward, however. I do not want to interfere in family matters which are of no concern to me."

"Do you not? What a pity. I think you should stay, though, for Edmund's sake, if not for your own."

"I do not understand you, sir."

"Surely you will not leave Edmund to my tender mercies? He is quite helpless, after all, and for all you know I might have a pistol in my pocket, or a stiletto! Or, at the very least, a handy piece of cord to strangle him with!"

"Cousin Alexander!" Edmund was torn between amusement and shame. "I never said—"

"You had no need to!" burst out Theodora, to Ravensworth's delight, abandoning her icy pose and flying into a passion. "One has only to look at him to see that he is cruel, and odious, and—and altogether shameless! And if you had found your poor ward alone and defenceless in the Forest, I think you would not be so flippant, Mr. Ravensworth!"

"Now, really, Miss Waverton—" began Edmund.

"No, no, let her be; it is most edifying! I had no idea I was so dangerous a character! It is well that you should be warned, Edmund."

Theodora was aware that she had strayed beyond the bounds of proper behaviour, and that her regrettable temper had led her to utter things that were not only downright slanderous, but also grossly exaggerated. She did not, indeed, believe that Ravensworth was the villain she had claimed him to be; nor, in his rational moments, did Edmund, as she had come to see. She blushed miserably.

"I beg your pardon," she said stiffly. "What I said was inexcusable."

"No, no, do not stop! It is not every day that one has a mirror held up to one's soul in this way!"

For the first time she looked fully at him, and he was suddenly ashamed of his teasing. He had forgotten the agonies and insecurities of her age, but the look on her face brought them back to him.

"I must ask you to accept my apology," she continued doggedly, and he admired the courage that made her speak.

"I do, though there is no need," he said more gently. "I should perhaps be apologising to you, for I was teasing you quite abominably."

Theodora was completely taken aback by his apology and his change of tone. She blushed again, looking adorably uncertain, and he found himself aching to take her in his arms and kiss the lips that were just curving into a doubtful smile. He stiffened. Kissing Miss Waverton, or even wanting to, was a habit he had no intention of getting into. To kiss a chance-met girl by the wayside was one thing; to kiss a gently brought-up girl while a guest in her mother's house could lead to complications of the most matrimonial kind, and he was far from wanting that.

"You said I should stay for my own sake as well?" questioned Theodora shyly when he did not speak. He was glad to break his chain of thought.

"Yes, indeed! If you had attempted to walk through the door at that moment, you would have been in the greatest danger of walking into something, or falling down the stairs! With your nose in the air, and looking down it as you were, you could not possibly have seen where you were going!"

She had to laugh, and the atmosphere lightened. A few minutes of more general conversation ensued, Mr. Ravensworth asking what the doctor had said, and giving news of Lady Lingdale, and of London acquaintances. Theodora had time to recover her composure, though she still felt unequal to joining in the talk, which was of people and places she did not know. At length she made a murmured excuse, and walked to the door.

Mr. Ravensworth was by this time standing by the bed, and this time when she went to leave the room he did not prevent her, reflecting that perhaps it was as well for his peace of mind that she should do so. Theodora stayed out of the way for as long as his visit lasted, and despised herself for watching him as he rode away. He did not visit again, but wrote saying that he was returning to London, since he was satisfied that his ward was receiving every care at the hands of his kind hostess.

It was early March before Lord Lingdale was able to leave his bed. Young and strong, he was horrified to find how weak he was after a few weeks in bed. Even his good leg would scarcely support him, and he found himself nervous of trusting any weight on the bad one, though the doctor assured him it had knit together again very well.

"You cannot expect to be dancing around straight away, after all," pointed out the doctor, to whom Edmund voiced his fears. "You must take things easily. The strength will soon come back to your muscles, but you cannot rush things. You might be itching to get back to London, but I am afraid you must remain here a while longer. Of course, there is nothing to stop you returning in a coach, and by easy stages, but you would do better to be guided by me, and spend another week or so here. Walk a little, as you feel like it, and increase the amount day by day. Little and often, that's the way."

Nothing loath, Edmund begged leave of his kind hostess to stay a while longer. Since he was by now more of an old friend than a guest, and she had found herself growing very fond of him, Lady Waverton could not deny him. Theodora was delighted—now Edmund could come down and spend his days in the sitting-room, and she could spend even more time with him.

Under these circumstances, it was inevitable that the two young people should have more opportunities to be alone together. Theodora scarcely noticed it, for she was quite unconscious of Edmund as a young man, but he rejoiced in it. Watching for his moment, he chose a time when Lady Waverton was likely to be absent for some time, and went to look for her. She welcomed him without surprise, though he usually spent the mornings in his room. They were sitting on the sofa together, she sewing, he supposedly writing, when he threw down his pen, and seized her hand in his.

"Be careful, Edmund," she admonished him absently. "I nearly ran the needle into my finger."

"I beg your pardon," he said, abashed, releasing his hold.

"Only a few more stitches. Why is it, I wonder, that the thread on one's needle always runs out when there is only a little way to go? There, it is done. Don't you think that's pretty?" She held up a square of cambric, finely embroidered in white work. "It is for Mama."

"Yes, very pretty. Theodora—?"

"It would never have done for me to have pricked my finger," she continued chattily, turning the handkerchief this way and that, "for blood, you know, is particularly hard to wash out of such work. I wonder whether I should put a few more leaves on to that wreath. What do you think?"

"For goodness' sake, Theodora, leave the wretched thing alone for a moment and listen to me!" begged her exasperated swain. Obediently she folded the work and turned towards him, hands in her lap, her face calmly interested.

"I beg your pardon, Edmund. I am attending now, truly. What did you want to say to me?"

He refused to let his unpropitious start dampen his ardour. Once again he grasped her hand in his, and held it firmly.

"Theodora," he began, "it cannot have escaped your notice that my feelings towards you, in the past weeks, have grown very warm."

"Oh, so have mine!" she exclaimed happily. "I have never had such a friend before, and it is so nice, and comfortable! And Mama is very fond of you, too!"

His carefully rehearsed periods flew from his mind.

"Dash it all, Dora, can't you let a fellow speak?"

"I beg your pardon, Edmund. I know I talk too much. Only, may I have my hand back? I still have my thimble on, and you are squeezing my fingers on it rather."

Once again he let go of her hand, and she removed the offending thimble, which slipped from her fingers and rolled across the carpet, disappearing instantly from sight as it became one with the pattern.

"Oh, dear, and it is Mama's best gold one! I am sorry, Edmund, but I must find it, for it could so easily be trodden on and ruined. Did you see where it went?"

She would have got down to the floor to look for it, but Edmund, gritting his teeth, forestalled her. On hands and knees he quartered the carpet, sweeping his hands across it until he found the missing thimble. Not bothering to rise, he brought it back to her, and put it in her lap.

"Oh, thank you, Edmund. How *very* obliging you are! I hope it doesn't hurt your leg, crawling like that. Won't you sit back here again now?"

She patted the sofa beside her, rather in the manner of one inviting a dog or a cat. Finding himself on his knees before her, he made the best of his opportunities. Taking her hand in his for the third time, he looked up at her.

"Oh, Theodora, I do love you," he said simply.

She was nonplussed. "You are not going to put a thimble on my finger, instead of a ring, are you?" she said shakily.

"Don't laugh at me, Dora! I mean it, I love you!"

"I didn't mean to laugh at you," she said in some distress. "I'm sorry, Edmund. This has never happened to me before."

"It has never happened to me either."

"Then how do you know it is really love?"

"How does anyone know? I dream of you, think of you night and day. Your voice is music in my ears . . ."

"That wasn't what you said yesterday," she murmured, with a twinkle. He ignored her levity.

"Music in my ears," he repeated firmly. "All I want is to be with you, forever. Oh, Dora, you must believe me!"

"I do! I do!" she said hastily. "Only, I don't wish to be unkind, Edmund, but do please get up off your knees! It cannot be good for your leg and, besides, anyone might come in."

"I don't care!" He was getting carried away. "I love you, and I don't care who knows it!"

"Well, I do. Why, what would Mama say if she should walk in now? She would not be very pleased with you, Edmund, and, though I shouldn't mention it, you owe her some return for her care of you."

"You are right; I should not have spoken to you without asking her permission first. I was carried away by my ardour."

It was true that his leg was aching, and he was not unwilling to rise from his knees and resume his place at her side. Theodora folded her hands firmly in her lap and fixed her eyes resolutely on him. Suddenly, they were both conscious of their mutual proximity. To sit side by side on a sofa, which before had been nothing, occasioned a new significance. Embarrassed, they each edged apart, until Theodora pulled herself together and gave a laugh.

"This is so ridiculous! We have often sat beside one another, and it has meant nothing. We may surely continue to do so now? Mama trusts you, I know, to behave as a gentleman should."

His face was clouded with gloom.

"I am sorry you find me ridiculous," he said.

"I did not say that! You must not mistake my meaning like that! Only, we were so comfortable together before, and it is a shame to spoil it."

"Have I spoiled things? I did not mean to."

"Not spoiled, exactly. But changed them. You must see that that is so."

"I thought that you felt as I do. I know I haven't known you for very long, but I really do love you, Dora."

"And I love you, too, but—"

He did not allow her to finish.

"You do? But that is wonderful! Oh, Dora, darling Dora, let me speak to your mother at once! You know, I have told my own mother all about you, so I do not think she will be surprised. She will be so delighted!"

He tried to take her into his arms, but she whisked herself away and was across the room before he could recover himself.

"Stop, Edmund, stop! I did not mean it!"

"Not mean it? You don't love me, then? Do not tease me, Dora, I can't bear it."

She came back to him then, and, seating herself beside him, took his hands in her own, holding them in a firm grip and forcing him to look at her.

"Edmund, listen to me. I don't mean to tease you. When I say that I love you, it is perfectly true, but I do not know that it is *that* kind of love. You are my good friend, my best friend, apart from Mama, and I love to be with you. I love you as much as any friend can love another, but as a *friend*. Do you see?"

"Isn't that enough?" he asked miserably.

She sighed. "Maybe it is. I think it is more than many married couples do feel for one another. But I don't know whether it is enough for me. You are the first young man I have ever known, and I am, I think, the first girl you have ever been friendly with, too. Don't you see that if we commit ourselves now we might be making a dreadful mistake? You will go back to London, and there will be many young ladies prettier and cleverer than I. How can you be sure you will not love one of them even more?"

"I won't. I know I won't. What you mean is, you might find someone better than me."

"I am sure I couldn't find anyone better," she said warmly. "Please don't be angry with me. I don't mean to hurt you." For the first time a tear sparkled in her eyes, and he was all contrition.

"Forgive me, Dora. You are wiser than I. Only don't cry!"

"I'm not, really," she sniffed, searching for her handkerchief. "Only I feel so confused, happy and sad all at once."

He patted her shoulder in a brotherly way, looking anxiously into her face until she smiled at him.

"It is not hopeless, then? You do not say you will never be mine?"

"Oh, no, not that. Oh, dear, it sounds so dreadfully coy and missish, but it is so sudden! I need time, that is all."

He was satisfied and had the tact to go and leave her alone. Lady Waverton, coming in a little while later, was told the whole, under a vow of silence, and they shared a laugh, not unkindly, over the hapless thimble-hunter.

"I have been afraid of something like this," admitted Lady Waverton, "but I did not see how it was to be avoided. To have kept you apart would have made things worse, I fear."

"Yes, it might. You do not dislike him, do you, Mama?"

"Not at all. He is a dear boy, and I must say that in some ways he is exactly the match I would have hoped for you. He is young, and kind, and loving, and I think you could have a happy life with him. But the last thing I want is for it to be said that he was entrapped into this marriage."

"Oh, Mama! Who could say such a thing?"

"The whole world would say it, if I were foolish enough to allow you two babies to engage yourselves to one another now. You have no idea how such gossip will spread. No, you did just as you should. I still hope to get you to London, for the Season. If, in a year or so, you can both say that you have found no one else you can be happy with, I will give you to him with a joyful heart."

Theodora was silent, but the memory of the one kiss she had received from Mr. Ravensworth could not be banished. It was true that Edmund had never attempted to kiss her. He was, she told herself, far too gentlemanly and respectful to attempt such an embrace without her permission. But she wondered, sometimes, whether she would have liked it if he had, and whether her feelings would have been the same as on that other occasion.

Nothing more was said on the subject, and, if Lady Waverton was more careful than before not to leave the young couple alone together, nobody remarked upon it. Lord Lingdale wrote a long letter to his mother, and three days later another letter, addressed to Lady Waverton, arrived from London.

Dear Lady Waverton,

Now that my dear Edmund is so much better, I feel I have been most remiss in not writing to you before. Your motherly heart will understand all that I have felt and suffered, knowing that my boy is in pain. Not for worlds, however, would I have inflicted my presence on your household, and Mr. Ravensworth has kept me well informed of your kind offices to my boy.

Edmund himself has written to me of your great goodness to him, and I feel it is only right to show my gratitude to you. Knowing something of your unfortunate circumstances, may I venture to suggest that you might find it convenient to send your dear little daughter to me, for a visit, while the Season is in progress? She is, I understand, just eighteen, and it is surely time she made her entrance into Society. I think I might say, without boasting, that I am acquainted with anyone worth knowing in the Metropolis, and you may be assured that I will guard her, and her interests, as if she had been my own.

I do hope, dear Lady Waverton, that my little suggestion will please you. It would certainly be a pleasure to me to have a young lady to present to the world and, with no daughters of my own, such a prospect has never come my way.

The letter closed with the usual compliments. Lady Waverton sat, frowning over it, for quite a while. It certainly seemed providential, and it was true that there was little other opportunity for Theodora to make her début, since her trustees, elderly gentlemen now, had been unable to suggest anything helpful. In the end, Lady Waverton said nothing to her daughter, but replied in forthright terms, saying that she had reason to think that Edmund was developing a romantic interest in Theodora. She felt it only right to warn Edmund's mother that her daughter would have only a small fortune.

Lady Lingdale called for the long-suffering Mr. Ravensworth again, and waved the letter at him. He read it in silence, his face expressionless.

"What do you think?" cried her ladyship in anxiety. "Is she very good, or just very clever?"

"Both, I should say," he replied, dropping the letter back into her lap.

"But what shall I do?"

"Carry on, and have the girl up here. You will win Edmund's gratitude and esteem, if nothing else. She is a pretty little thing, and has been well brought up. You will have nothing to blush for in her."

"But she might have her head turned, and fall in love with someone else. After all, if she is Jonas Bellerby's heiress, she will have them after her like bees round a honey-pot."

"It is not generally known that they are related. And do not forget that it is by no means a certain thing. I did not say she was his heiress—only that she might be."

"It is all so very complicated," she fluttered. "I do not know what to do for the best."

"Bring her to London and have done with it. If nothing else, you will enjoy taking her about. They are not too well off, I suspect. She will need dressing. You may draw on me for funds, and let her think you are paying, out of gratitude for saving Edmund."

She looked at him in amazement.

"If I did not know you better, I should say you were hanging out after the girl yourself," she said suspiciously.

"Is it likely?" he drawled. "Have I ever shown an interest in eighteen-year-old *ingénues* before? You will have to put it down to my own gratitude, for saving my ward."

"I never thought you so fond of him."

"Did you not? But then, I always said you were too fond, didn't I? Perhaps I was just redressing the balance," he replied callously, and left before she could think of an answer.

His actual reasons for encouraging Lady Lingdale to bring Theodora to London he was not, at that moment, prepared to examine. Certainly, the idea of young Edmund making love to her filled him with rage. After all, he thought, the boy was too young to be fixing his interest yet, and to a penniless girl at that. He did not for a moment think it likely that Theodora had fallen in love with him.

From his memories of his own calf-love, he thought it likely that Edmund would get over it far more quickly if the girl were here, with his mother, than if she were some distant romantic memory, the fabled princess of the fairy tales in her forest bower. And if he, himself, were to see her more often, perhaps he would not find her drifting into his thoughts so frequently. Sometimes, when he was off guard, he had caught himself noting something amusing, and thinking that she would laugh at it when he told her. He was spending less time at his club, for somehow cards and games of chance seemed less interesting than before, but when he attended balls or assemblies he found himself comparing the insipid beauties with whom he danced or conversed to Theodora, to their disadvantage. Decidedly, he needed to see her in this London setting where he was so at home. He would soon see that she was gauche, and countrified, and probably not as pretty as he remembered her, either.

CHAPTER SIX

"To London? With Lady Lingdale? Oh, Mama!" Theodora clasped her hands together, as if to contain the excitement that bubbled within her. "But when? When am I to go?"

"About the middle of next week. It will then be nearly the end of March and, if you are to make your début at the beginning of the Season, in May, you will only just have enough time."

"But... my clothes! I have nothing suitable—at least, not for London!"

Lady Waverton laughed.

"Of course you have not, silly goose! That is what I meant. You will need at least two weeks, when you arrive, to order clothes. Lady Lingdale tells me I may rely on her to guide your choice, and I know she may be trusted, for she is very fashionable, though she does not entertain a great deal."

"But Mama, the expense! Have you thought? For I will need several day dresses, and I suppose at least two for evening wear! How is it to be managed?"

"Rather more than two, I hope, or you will present a very shabby appearance. My love, I have been saving for just this occasion for a very long time. Better not to appear at all, than to appear poorly dressed! Your trustees are prepared to advance a sum, and I myself have quite a lot more put by. I did not spend all the money I received when I sold my jewels, and with part of what I have been able to make by my writing there is enough to give you a creditable appearance. I may rely on you, I know, to be sensible, and take care of your things, but remember that it is a false economy to buy too cheap! Let your clothes be simple, but the material of the first quality, and above all buy good gloves, and bonnets, and footwear."

Theodora, silenced for once, listened in amazement to this wise advice. To one who was accustomed to wear only the simplest and most practical of garments, the vista that was opening out before her was almost stunning.

"Jewels, fortunately, are not much worn just now. I am glad: nothing looks worse, to my mind, than to see a young girl decked out in sparkling stones—so vulgar. There is a pretty set of pearl ornaments that I had as a girl that will be just the thing, however, and I do have a very nice fan, of ivory, that you may take as well. Do not stare at me like that! As I told you, I have been planning for this moment for years! I never expected you to be so lucky as to make your début under the aegis of anyone like Lady Lingdale, though. Really, we have a great deal to be thankful for."

She saw that tears were flowing down her daughter's cheeks.

"Oh Mama! I have never been away from you before! How will I manage without you?"

"My dear child, you quite worry me when you talk like this! Of course you will miss me, a little, but you will be enjoying yourself so much! Think of the fun you will be having! It is time you went out into the world, and lived a little."

"But you will be lonely down here!" Theodora flung herself into her mother's arms and sobbed. Lady Waverton resolutely swallowed a tightness in her throat.

"Well, of course I shall miss you," she said judiciously, "but I have plenty to occupy me, you know. I mean to go out and about more in the village, when you

are away. There are several long-standing invitations,
which until now I have always refused, that I mean to take
up. Then I shall expect you to write me long letters, telling
me what you are doing, and whom you have met, and
where. How I shall enjoy them!''

Theodora allowed herself to be comforted and distracted, and the next few days were so busy that she had no
time for fears of the future. Edmund, too, was delighted,
and only too happy to describe to her all the delights of
London. Mr. Ravensworth was sending his own carriage,
coachman and footmen to convey them, and Edmund assured her that, while it may not have a crest on the panel,
it was far smarter and more comfortable than anything of
his mother's, while his horses were second to none. They
were to travel slowly, not to tire Edmund—at his mother's
behest, and greatly to his shame—which meant that they
would be at least six or seven hours on the journey, for the
Sussex roads, in particular, were notoriously bad, especially at this time of year. They would halt at an inn for a
meal at midday, much to Theodora's excitement. She had
never been to an inn.

"You will take Mary with you, as your maid," decreed
Lady Waverton. "She is a good creature, and will take
good care of your clothes. As to your hair, I hope that
Lady Lingdale will see that you have it fashionably
dressed. If Mary cannot learn to do it for you, Lady Lingdale's maid might do so, in which case you must be sure to
make her a present."

"I shall never remember everything!"

"Nonsense! You have plenty of common sense—just use
it!"

All the common sense she possessed, however, was not
enough to prevent Theodora weeping again at the moment of departure. To say an actual farewell to her mother
was beyond her; a convulsive hug, and one last kiss, and

she dived into the carriage, determined not to make a spectacle of herself in public. Fortunately Mary was made of sterner stuff, and was herself so excited at the trip that before they had gone many miles Theodora was able to smile again, and exclaim at the changing countryside they were going through. Edmund was in the highest of spirits, and the first half of the journey passed swiftly.

Luncheon, at the inn, was everything that Theodora had hoped for. Not only was the building charmingly quaint, but she actually was able to witness the arrival of a mail coach, and see the travellers, inside and out, rushing into the building to snatch what refreshments they might swallow while the horses were being changed. It was very romantic, of course, particularly when the driver whipped up the horses, and the coach swept out of the yard. All the same, eyeing the pinched blue faces of those unfortunates who had outside seats, she was very thankful to return to the space and comfort of Ravensworth's coach, with a freshly heated brick by her feet, and no draughts coming through the well-made doors.

It was dusk by the time they reached London, and Theodora was very tired. Not too tired, however, to strain her eyes through the windows—Edmund would not consider opening them, for he was now cold and, truth to tell, rather grumpy. His innate good nature, however, was not proof against Theodora's bubbling spirits, and he obligingly tried to identify such places of interest as they passed. Theodora, who had never in her life been farther than East Grinstead, was astonished at the size of London. She knew, of course, that it was a great city, but they seemed to have been driving forever, through streets of houses, and yet Edmund assured her they were still not there!

At last some familiar landmarks told him that they were approaching Mount Street. The excited Mary began to fuss over the many small items of luggage that were in the car-

riage, but Theodora fell silent. All at once she realised the
enormity of what was happening to her, and she would
have given anything to be transported, by some helpful
genie, back to the safety of home, and her mother.

In the bustle of arrival it was Edmund, of course, who
was naturally foremost in his mother's eyes. It was not
until she had greeted, embraced, and scolded him, and
shed a few happy tears, that she was free to notice the small
figure of Theodora, waiting shyly in the background, her
eyes blinking in the light of what seemed to her to be mil-
lions of candles. Mr. Ravensworth, who for reasons of his
own had chosen to be present at the arrival, kept himself
out of the way, and Theodora had not noticed him. At last
Lady Lingdale turned to greet her guest.

"My dear Miss Waverton! Forgive a mother's fond
partiality, that I have ignored you so long!"

Theodora, abashed at finding herself in a hall that was
grander by far than any room she had ever seen in her life,
dropped a schoolgirl's curtsy, looking with open admiration at the evening gown of straw-coloured satin, with an
overdress of ivory gauze, which Lady Lingdale had put on
as sufficiently fine for an evening at home—though not,
of course, good enough for going out, for it was far from
new. The reflection of Edmund's handsome face was seen
in her own, while her hair was still a determined shade of
gold, and though she had in recent years put on a great
deal of weight she was still a good-looking woman.

"And after all," she had said to a good friend, "with the
Regent growing so large, not to mention Mrs. Fitzherbert—not that I do mention her, unless I have to—who can
complain if the rest of us are plump?" To which the friend,
whose own figure had also spread, had given hearty
agreement.

"Put off that dreadful cloak, my dear," said her ladyship, "and let me look at you."

Theodora opened her mouth to say that this was, in fact, her best cloak, and quite new, when she caught Edmund's anguished eye, and closed her lips. More from what Edmund had not said, than from what he had, she had gathered that it was of the first importance not to argue with his mama, and indeed her own mother had told her that Lady Lingdale's dicta on the subject of clothes were to be taken as law.

She therefore meekly laid aside the maligned garment, and stood with unusual patience while her hostess considered her, eyes narrowed. Blushing a little, she lifted her chin and stiffened her knees, which had a betraying tendency to wobble, which she attributed, hopefully, to tiredness. Ravensworth, who from his chosen place in the adjoining room could see her reflection in the large mirror over the chimney-piece, smiled.

"You are not very tall; it is a pity," pronounced Lady Lingdale. "Still, your figure is good, and your skin, thank heaven, is clear, and not disfigured by too much sunshine. The gown, of course, is quite impossible." Theodora, who had watched her own mother labour over the sewing, felt a prickle of tears behind her eyes, but clenched her teeth until her jaws ached to keep them down. Lady Lingdale came closer, and Theodora subdued an impulse to shrink back as she picked up a lock of hair which, as usual, had escaped from its moorings.

"Are the curls natural? Good. Open your mouth, child." Feeling more and more like a beast at market, Theodora did as she was bidden. "Excellent teeth! Nothing is worse than a girl who may not open her mouth to speak or smile without displaying gaps or blackened teeth. Show me your hands."

Theodora, who had been making a severe effort not to bite her nails, and had also been applying Mag's cream assiduously, held them out. Lady Lingdale took one, and examined it.

"Good heavens, girl! Never tell me you bite them?"

As she had feared, a week or two of care was not sufficient to hide the bad habit of years. For the first time Theodora hung her head.

"I am very sorry, my lady. I have tried to stop, and I will not do so in future. My mama made me promise..." An unwelcome tear trickled down her cheek, and Lady Lingdale, who was not a cruel woman, was softened.

"I did not mean to scold you, my dear! And your hands at least are soft, and ladylike in other respects. You will scarcely be able to appear in public for at least a week, until you have some clothes fit to be seen in—and my woman is very clever. Besides, you will be wearing gloves, and they will hide a multitude of sins."

Theodora achieved a wobbly smile.

"I should tell you, Lady Lingdale, how grateful I am for your invitation. I shall do my very best to please you, and I hope I will not cause you too much bother."

"Dear child! You may give me a kiss!" As Theodora, watched with a happy look by Edmund, availed herself of this honour, Lady Lingdale took her by the hand to lead her out of the hall.

"You must come and rest, for I am sure you must be exhausted! Nothing is more tiring than travelling, and I am invariably afflicted with a severe headache after spending as little as one hour in a carriage, let alone almost a whole day! You must allow me to tell you how happy I am to hear that you have no unfortunate country mannerisms in your speech! I know that Ravensworth assured me that your speech was well-bred, but I was still a little anxious."

"Mr. Ravensworth told you that? How very obliging of him." Theodora's voice had a little edge to it, and at that moment they passed into the downstairs sitting-room, where Ravensworth took his ease in a chair by the fire.

"Yes, wasn't it? Good evening, Miss Waverton. I hope you have not had too unpleasant a journey?"

He rose, and her eyes widened as she took in the full glory of his evening attire. Hitherto she had seen him only in riding dress, but now his black silk knee breeches, silk stockings, and black coat would have informed the initiated that he was dining out. He had given no thought to his appearance; it was merely his normal mode of dress, for he dined with friends or at his club on most evenings. Theodora, however, assumed that he wanted to impress, and reacted accordingly.

"Thankye, sir. I disremember if ever I was in so fine a carriage. Proper vlothered, I be, sir."

His lips twitched, Edmund gave a shout of laughter, but Lady Lingdale emitted a well-bred scream of anguish.

"Miss Waverton! And to think I was so pleased that you spoke well! One can scarcely understand a word you say!"

"I beg your pardon, ma'am. I am afraid I forgot myself."

"Then make sure you do not do so again! I was never so shocked in my life!"

"Do not scold her," said Ravensworth lazily. "I fancy she meant only to give me a set-down. Quite good, Miss Waverton, but do not forget that I still owe you a spanking!"

"You lay a finger on her at your peril, guardian or no guardian," retorted Edmund, firing up at once in defence of his beloved.

"Take no notice, Edmund. Mr. Ravensworth is merely teasing me," she told him.

"He has no business to do so!"

"No, of course not. But it is far more dignified to ignore his impertinence," she informed him sweetly. Edmund fell into a simmering silence.

"Very good, Miss Waverton!" applauded Ravensworth, in no way put out. "I see you will be able to hold your own in any society. My congratulations, Cousin Amelia, on having acquired so charming and lively a companion. I feel sure that she will be a success."

He walked to where Theodora, silently fuming, stood, and lifted her chin with one white finger. "Do not allow them to turn you into a pretty, subdued clothes-horse," he advised her, "and do not be afraid to say what you think—within reason, of course! The occasional use of dialect might bring you the reputation of being an original, which will do you no harm indeed."

"I am so grateful for your good opinion," she said venomously, "but I feel sure that I would do better to prefer Lady Lingdale's advice to yours. My mother says she is of the first rank of fashion."

He smiled gently.

"There, that is just what I meant! A little gauche, but I am sure you will improve with practice." He patted her cheek, in an odiously patronising way, and left.

"Well! I do not believe I have ever heard anyone speak to Alexander like that!" said Lady Lingdale, between admiration and horror. "Whatever possessed you, child?"

"I beg your pardon, ma'am. I am afraid I behaved badly. But there is something about Mr. Ravensworth that brings out the worst side of my nature."

"I know what you mean. He can be very annoying but, all the same, I do not think you should address him like that again."

"I think she did just right," put in the loyal Edmund. "It is time that someone took Cousin Ravensworth down a peg."

"But only consider, Edmund! Of course I am pleased that Lady Waverton should have said what she did about me, and I flatter myself that is not altogether untrue, but Ravensworth has such influence! Far more than I do, and a word from him would be enough to make you a success, or completely unfashionable!"

"Is he really so important? I had no idea. He has no title, after all."

"No, but he is very well-connected. One of his grandmothers was a Duchess. Besides, titles mean nothing nowadays. Only look at Mr. Brummell! He is far more important than the Regent, even."

"Yes, I know. But Mr. Brummell is unique, is he not?"

"Of course. But when I tell you that Ravensworth dines with him..."

Theodora was appalled, but hid it successfully. "Then I suppose I must follow his advice, as well as yours, ma'am. One thing is certain: I shall not allow him to browbeat me!" Lady Lingdale regarded her with trepidation. Edmund successfully turned the subject by asking how his mother proposed to entertain their guest during the coming week.

"Need you ask? We shall be shopping, of course! The modiste first thing in the morning, naturally. We shall have to be out early, for I do not want too many people to see you in your country clothes, my love! Then, of course, there will be hats, and bonnets, and shoes, and gloves...and I must have the hairdresser here, as soon as may be."

Edmund looked glum.

"I had thought I might take Theodora to see some of the sights," he said. "You know she has never seen London before."

"How kind of you! I do so look forward to setting eyes on St. Paul's and the Tower, and everything! But I would not like you to be ashamed of me, or to embarrass your mama!''

"I could never be ashamed of you," he responded gallantly.

"If she is not too tired, you may take her for a drive round tomorrow afternoon, in a closed carriage," Lady Lingdale allowed graciously. "But she is not to appear in public just yet. We are going to astonish them, my dear!"

Theodora found her head almost reeling with excitement at this heady prospect, and acknowledged that she would like to do so. Sternly repressed within her was the thought that, above all, she would like to astonish Mr. Ravensworth. By now her eyes were closing of their own accord, and she was grateful to find herself taken upstairs to the most luxurious bedchamber she had ever seen. A light supper, from a tray, was soon disposed of, and contrary to her expectations she fell asleep almost before she had finished saying her prayers, and certainly before the pangs of homesickness had time to make themselves felt.

The following morning, much refreshed, she was carried off by her hostess to the fashionable modiste at the back of Bond Street that Lady Lingdale herself patronised. To Theodora's secret relief, that urbane and terrifying lady made no comment upon her clothes, nor did she demand that she open her mouth or display her hands. Instead she cast knowing eyes over the neat figure, the white skin, and the shining mass of chestnut curls, and allowed a small but gratified smile to appear on her subtly painted face.

"It will be a pleasure to dress Mademoiselle," she said simply, "as it has always been a pleasure to dress milady." Seating her customers on small gilt chairs, she summoned with one flick of her fingers what seemed, to Theodora's bemused gaze, an endless procession of elegantly clad ladies.

"White, just white, or the very palest of colours, for her first Season," decreed Lady Lingdale, and unerringly steered her dazzled charge away from the spangled gauzes and figured lace that drew her eye. Theodora recalled her mother's advice, and shyly agreed to the lengths of fine muslin—plain and sprigged—cambric, and silk, for morning and afternoon dresses.

"We will have a wrap-over bodice for the muslins, and the cambric, with a little fullness at the back," pronounced Lady Lingdale decidedly. "I think the new style, instead of those deep-set sleeves, much more graceful, for the narrow back held one so very stiff! A muslin antique ruff, I think, for the neck of the dimity, and tuckers for the rest. Long sleeves, of course, for day wear, and no more than a little flounce, or some fine embroidery in the Grecian style, at the wrist. The blue spencer, without a doubt, and I liked that military pelisse of amber velvet. Military styles are so much in vogue, but I am not sure about the colour."

The modiste suggested, with becoming humility, that with Mademoiselle's colouring, green would be almost indispensable.

"Very good." Lady Lingdale was pleased to agree. "And we must find some half-boots to match. Now, for the evening dresses . . . What is it, dear child?" Theodora was attempting, in some distress, to attract her attention.

"Lady Lingdale, if I might have a word…" She cast an anguished glance at Madame, who tactfully recalled something she must see to elsewhere. "Lady Lingdale, I am very grateful to you for all your trouble, but I think this must be a very expensive place! You know, Mama is not very rich, and, though she has been most generous to me, I must be careful how much I spend! Do I really need all this?"

"It seems a great deal, I know," agreed her ladyship sympathetically, "but I do assure you that you cannot forever be appearing in the same gown, day after day! What we buy this week should last you for the whole of the Season, I hope, and you must regard it, as I am sure your mama would do, as an investment. As for your evening gowns, I should very much like to make you a gift of them."

"Lady Lingdale, you are too kind, but I could not possibly accept—"

"Now I do not want to hear another word, unless you mean seriously to wound my sensibilities. I owe you Edmund's health, if not his very life, and nothing could repay you for that. It gives me pleasure to see you looking your best, and I shall be most hurt if you refuse me this small thing." Lady Lingdale understood, none better, the art of ruling by weakness and, when she drew out her handkerchief and raised it to her eyes, Theodora found that she could not continue to argue.

In the end an order was placed for a white satin underdress, which as Lady Lingdale pointed out might be worn with several different overdresses. These were commanded in white gauze, the palest of green tiffany, and a rather daring shell-pink tarlatan.

"With hair of your chestnut colouring, that just escapes being red, I think you may safely wear it," opined her ladyship.

With great good fortune, it was discovered that Madame had in readiness a walking dress of muslin, with a blue pelisse of Levantine twilled silk, which would require very little alteration to fit Mademoiselle. Madame promised that these would be delivered to Mount Street the very next day, and that the other garments would be put in hand with the utmost celerity.

Even with Lady Lingdale's help, the sum mentioned, in the most genteel undertone, by Madame, was enough to take away Theodora's breath, although she succeeded in betraying no more than a well-bred lack of interest. Lady Lingdale fixed Madame with a stern eye.

"I should tell you, I think, that my young cousin, Mr. Ravensworth, himself recommended that I should take in hand Miss Waverton's début. I need hardly tell you that, with her face and figure, and his approval, I expect her to be one of the foremost belles of the season. Naturally, we should like to be able to say that all her gowns came from you, but one must consider the practicalities..."

Her voice trailed off thoughtfully, and Madame, not blind to the fact that the young lady would be a walking advertisement for her, obligingly recalled that, during March, it was her custom to make a substantial reduction to such valued customers as dear Lady Lingdale had always been. The new figure was amicably agreed, and Lady Lingdale swept her protégée out of the door.

"Excellent," she said, as they seated themselves once more in the carriage. "I own I did not expect her to come down so much. It just goes to show, my dear, that Alexander Ravensworth has his uses." It also showed, she thought but did not say, that her son's guardian was probably quite right in prophesying a social success for her young charge—women such as the modiste had an unerring eye for such things.

Well satisfied though she was with the morning's work, Lady Lingdale professed herself quite worn out, and far too tired to do any more shopping until the following day. Since it was unthinkable that Theodora should be allowed to choose anything so crucial as a bonnet without her guidance, she was given permission to drive out with Edmund in the afternoon, while his mama recruited her strength on the sofa.

The outing was a success, though Theodora several times found herself feeling a little irritated by her escort's lack of knowledge. Expert though he was on the classics, and on ancient writers, he had nothing at all to say about such newcomers as Lord Byron, who was beginning to be much talked about, but whom Edmund stigmatised as a self-opinionated dandy. Nor was Edmund able to tell her much about the famous buildings they drove round, though had they been visiting Rome, or the Parthenon, he would doubtless have been very informative.

A little disappointed, Theodora turned the subject to a fascinating conversation she had enjoyed with Lady Lingdale earlier in the day.

"Is it true, do you think, that Mr. Brummell and the Regent have quite fallen out? Your mama was saying, this morning, that it was."

"Was she? I do not know. I am afraid I have always found such things too trivial to be of interest." Theodora laughed and teased him for behaving like an elderly misanthrope, but she was not altogether displeased, on their return, to find Mr. Ravensworth sitting with her hostess. Quite forgetting his disagreeable behaviour of the night before, in her thirst for knowledge, she applied to him for information.

"Prinny and the Beau? Yes, it is certainly true. I am afraid our Regent is a changeable friend, and, while he can be the most charming man in the world, one can never rely on his favour's continuing."

"But there must be some reason? What can have happened?" Lady Lingdale was also longing for news.

"There are several versions. One theory is that Brummell, at Lady Jersey's house, called for *Mistress* Fitzherbert's carriage, which upset the lady and her Royal friend." Lady Lingdale cast a warning glance towards Theodora, who coloured.

"Have no fear, ma'am. I have heard about Mrs. Fitzherbert and the Prince."

"Yes. Well, there is also the nickname Brummell coined for them. He called Prinny 'Ben,' after one of the porters at Carlton House who is inordinately fat, and the lady 'Benina.' "

"Ben and Benina! Well, it would be enough to enrage the Regent. All the world knows how sensitive he is about his size."

"True, though I don't believe all of this. The trouble is, stories collected around Brummell like bees around a honeypot, and half of them are untrue. He can be sarcastic, I know, but I have never known him to be as rude as all that. No, I think the truth is, they are such different characters, *au fond* that they were bound to drift apart. Brummell does not care for Prinny's friends, nor his morals, nor his manners. What will become of it all, will remain to be seen."

"Can Mr. Brummell afford to slight the Prince?"

"At the moment, I think he may. He is acknowledged everywhere as the arbiter of taste, the leader of Society. But can it last? I wouldn't like to hazard a guess. The Regent is, after all, Monarch in all but name, and that will come—if he doesn't die of heart failure, or explode—before the King should die."

"Such a shame," mourned Lady Lingdale. "He was such a handsome young man!"

"Handsome is as handsome does," retorted her cousin, and would not be drawn on the subject any further.

CHAPTER SEVEN

THE SUBSEQUENT WEEK passed by in a flurry of activity. Bonnets and hats, silk stockings and parasols, half-boots and slippers of kid, or of white satin for evening wear, must all be bought. Lady Lingdale bethought her of another problem: did Theodora know how to dance? Her guest admitted that her knowledge was more theoretical than practical, and at once her ladyship engaged the daily services of a dancing master, saying firmly that it would do Edmund no harm at all to gain some practice by partnering her.

Edmund, however, was sadly absent-minded, and when called to order could give as excuse only that he had been seeking for the exact word to describe the colour of her eyes, or the curl of her hair. Theodora was bound to find this flattering, but at the same time she wished he would concentrate more on the movement of the dance. Ravensworth, who had several times called on them, arrived during just such a session.

"For heaven's sake, Edmund! How will the poor girl ever learn to dance if you cannot even concentrate?"

"I am sure Edmund is doing his best," Theodora at once fired up in defence of her partner. "After all, he has had a broken leg, you know, and I think the fault was mine."

"Yes, it was," he agreed annoyingly, "but the whole point of the exercise is that he should be able to help you through such difficulties! Here, let me show you."

To her horror he firmly disengaged her hands, which clutched on to Edmund.

"Be careful, Dora! You will crease my sleeve, and this is a new coat!"

"Come now, Miss Waverton, you may have him back directly!" The older man's voice was the soothing tone one might use to a small child, or a lunatic, and reluctantly Theodora allowed him to lead her into the dance. The hired musician struck a chord on the pianoforte, and she found herself taken through the movements with an ease she had not hitherto experienced. She had to admit that, with Ravensworth imperceptibly impelling her in the right direction, the steps were easier to remember.

As they reached the bottom of the imaginary set, he swept her into his arms. Theodora felt the heat of her burning cheeks as she breathed that familiar smell of Russia leather that hung about his person, but nothing could have been more impersonal than his manner.

"Now, for this once, I will count out loud, so—one, and two, and...no, other foot, Miss Waverton. And again, one, and two...better. No, it scarcely hurts at all," he said kindly in response to her muttered apology. "You are at least more daintily shod than at our previous meeting..."

"How unfair!" she shot at him. "No gentleman would remind me of that, at such a moment!"

"But I thought you had already decided I was no gentleman?" he quizzed her, whirling her round the corner until her feet almost left the ground and she felt herself almost solely supported by his strong hand at her back.

"If I had not already done so, I must now have been sure!" she returned crossly, when she had her breath back.

"There, now, I think you have it, do you not?" he smiled at her. She realised that the dance was at an end, and they were standing by Lady Lingdale, who was torn between pleasure at seeing that Theodora was learning properly, and irritation at the implied criticism of Edmund.

"Thank you, Alexander, very prettily done, indeed. I think Theodora will be all right now."

"Yes, but will I?" he said, too low for anyone but his partner to hear.

"I was particularly pleased to see that you were managing to converse, Theodora," continued Lady Lingdale. "Nothing is worse than to see young people having to concentrate so hard on their feet that they never remember to say a word! A gentleman requires to be entertained, you know!"

"Yes, poor things," commiserated Theodora. "I hope I did not bore you, Mr. Ravensworth?"

"Not at all. Your conversation was most entertaining and—er—instructive, Miss Waverton."

He bowed over her hand, and took himself off. Just for once, she thought, it would be so very pleasant to be able to have the last word!

After almost ten days of consolidated effort, Lady Lingdale pronounced herself satisfied. For her charge's first appearance, she had chosen a small party given by one of her intimate friends, who was herself bringing out her eldest daughter that same Season, and wanted to provide a not too intimidating introduction to the polite world.

Theodora, outwardly calm but inwardly in turmoil, allowed herself plenty of time to get ready. The hairdresser, called in by Lady Lingdale, had refused to allow scissors near her hair, but had dressed it in a heavy knot, high up on her head, that emphasised the length of her neck. The two or three curls that he allowed to fall, with artful negligence, lay like burnished chestnuts against her white skin, and a simple filet of white ribbon, together with two small white hothouse rosebuds, completed the masterpiece.

For her gown, Lady Lingdale had decreed the white satin slip, with the white gauze overdress. Mama's pearl necklace round her throat, the matching studs in her ears and bracelet outside her elbow-length kid gloves, made her feel truly grown-up, while Mama's fan of carved-and-pierced ivory, newly cleaned with milk, lent a final, elegant touch.

Theodora stood for several minutes before the cheval glass, less out of vanity than to give herself courage. Never, in her whole life, had she worn so low-cut a gown; she felt strangely exposed and naked, and noticed with some surprise that she could see the movement of her own heartbeat, pounding with nerves. One last glance, to remember to describe to Mama, and she turned resolutely to the door.

Edmund, at the foot of the stairs, let his mouth fall open in admiration as she trod, enveloped in a scented cloud of Hungary Water, down to the hall.

"My goodness, Dora, you look beautiful!" he exclaimed.

"So do you," she replied with some truth, eyeing the new knee-breeches of black silk, and the cut of his black coat.

"Meyer's, in Conduit Street," he informed her with simple pride.

"Of course," she replied with becoming gravity.

"I am glad to see that you are both ready," interrupted his mother, sweeping down the stairs in her turn. "Nothing is more annoying than unpunctuality." She herself had chosen, for once, to look matronly, and was opulently gowned in purple silk, with a matching turban and feathers. She inspected Theodora from all angles, adjusted the position of one of the rosebuds, and pronounced herself satisfied.

"Very pretty," she said judiciously, "and exactly the right style—neither too young, nor too sophisticated."

"It is all thanks to you, ma'am," said Theodora with gratitude.

"Well, maybe, but, no matter how good the clothes, it is not everyone who can wear them. Come, now, it is time we were going. Remember, Theodora, not to dance more than twice with any gentleman, even Edmund, no matter how you are importuned. You would not like to be labelled fast."

"Oh, no," Theodora shuddered. "But Lady Lingdale, suppose nobody asks me to dance?"

Edmund cried out at this, and Lady Lingdale smiled.

"I think that is unlikely to happen," she said.

When Theodora sat down the following day to write to her mama, she found that, try as she might, the first hour of the party had left no impression on her mind beyond those of light, noise, movement, and above all, anxiety. Her cheeks burning like fire, but hands and feet cold as ice, she had answered the kindly greetings of her hostess like some kind of automaton. The daughter of the house, a girl of her own age, was already surrounded by a group of talking, laughing young people, for as one of a large family she had a network of cousins, friends, and acquaintances already.

Theodora had stood, eyes blurred with panic, by Lady Lingdale, replying to that lady's remarks with random words and smiles. Understanding, dimly, how she must be feeling, Lady Lingdale quickly sent her off to dance with Edmund. At first she was confused by the crowds; it was one thing to practise with Edmund or the dancing master in the relative space of the Mount Street drawing-room, but quite another to be surrounded by so many other couples, most of them conversing in that clear, carrying tone that was the prerogative of the English ruling class, and which almost drowned the music.

Edmund, however, was a familiar partner, and gradually her initial panic had subsided, as she found her body automatically carrying out the movements she had so painstakingly learned. At least if she made a mistake, no one in such a crowd was likely to notice it, she thought.

She was not to know that more than one pair of eyes had been fixed, speculatively, upon her. The entrance of Lady Lingdale, and her adored only son, with a young lady who bid fair to be the prettiest girl in the room, had excited not a little interest. A little ripple of enquiry ran round the crowd, which her ladyship feigned not to notice, but, when it was found that nobody knew who she was, one enterprising mother of two hopeful sons was moved to seek enlightenment.

"What a delightful girl Lord Lingdale's partner is! She arrived with you, I think?"

"Yes, a charming child. I am so enjoying taking her about; I never realised before what I was missing by not having a daughter."

"Quite. I did not catch her name?"

"Miss Waverton. Theodora Waverton. Such a large name, as I say to her, for so petite a person! In fun, of course. Theodora has *such* a sense of humour!"

"Quite so. An invaluable asset. Miss Waverton . . . the name seems a little familiar, but I do not know . . ."

"You may perhaps recall her father, Sir George Waverton? Rather before my time, of course . . ." mused Lady Lingdale, who was enjoying herself.

"A family connection?" Indefatigable in the search for gossip, her companion was not one to take affront too easily.

"No, but a good friend. Her mother, Lady Waverton— a delightful woman—and I have corresponded for, oh, I do not know how long!" At this moment Lady Lingdale perceived another friend across the room. "You will excuse me, I know, for I have just seen Emily Weston, and I have not spoken to her for an age!''

She drifted across the room, and was soon deep in conversation again. She had the satisfaction of knowing that she had revealed as little as possible under interrogation, for she knew only too well that nothing created more interest than a touch of mystery. To her friend she was more forthcoming.

"What a very handsome couple they make together, Edmund and his partner! Is she the pretty little stranger everyone is talking about?''

"I suppose so. Is everyone wondering about her? It is no great mystery, after all. She is the daughter of Sir George Waverton; you may recall the unfortunate story of his wife, when we were no more than young wives ourselves! Poor thing, I always pitied her.''

"Yes, I remember now. Very young, wasn't she? I remember my mother saying how shocking she thought it—a marriage of May and December, she called it. And this is the daughter? I hope she may manage to live down the scandal.''

"But surely, so long ago . . . ?''

"There are always a few people with long memories and longer tongues. You must not hope for too much, unless . . . Is there any fortune? That would make all the difference.''

This was the question Lady Lingdale had been hoping to avoid. On the one hand, she wanted to present Theodora in the best possible light, but on the other, she had no desire to see Edmund's chances spoiled by the attentions of the numerous attractive, impecunious members of the ton who would undoubtedly flock round if Theodora were known to be an heiress.

"No, not a fortune,'' she said at length, unwillingly. "She is not penniless, of course, but her father gambled nearly everything away. She will have a few thousand, no more.''

''Better than nothing, but not enough for anything out of the way, unless she is very lucky. Is Edmund *épris?*''

It was impossible to deny it, for everyone must see the proud, possessive look on his face as they danced.

''Well, I believe he is. But it may well be that nothing will come of it.''

If the Hon. Mrs. Weston was surprised to learn that her friend was prepared to countenance a match between the apple of her eye, Edmund, and a girl of slightly dubious ancestry and no more than a modest fortune to go with her undoubtedly pretty face, she did not say so. Nevertheless, during the next few weeks, rumour somehow got round that the lovely Miss Waverton, though her hostess denied it, was in some way an heiress.

Ravensworth, when applied to for information, merely looked saturnine, and smiled. There were enough people, however, who recalled young Lady Waverton's marriage, and the name of her uncle and guardian. It was not long before the connection was made, and Theodora was whispered to be an heiress.

Theodora's fears were rapidly seen to be unfounded. No sooner had her dance with Edmund finished than she was obliged to choose between no less than three young men, all clamouring for an introduction and a chance to lead her into the next set. Without any embarrassment she at once picked one by the unusual, if effective, expedient of a child's counting-out rhyme, which had all of them laughing, and sent the two losers away without rancour.

It was with some difficulty that Edmund was able to claim his right to take her down to supper, where he sat her firmly by his mama while he fetched them plates of delicacies, the look on his face strongly reminiscent of a dog guarding a bone. As he, knowing his Theodora's appetite,

heaped her plate with lobster patties, chicken in aspic, sa-
voury pastries, and other delights, he was aware of a small
ripple of excitement running round the room. Glancing
towards the door, he saw the tall figure of his guardian,
while standing beside him was the dapper, sublimely elegant being that even he, with his lack of interest in the do-
ings of the ton, could not fail to recognise.

"The Beau! Heavens above!" he murmured to himself,
and made his way back to Lady Lingdale.

His mother, with a wisdom that he was not able to ap-
preciate until later, gave him a piercingly direct look that
gave an order as clearly as if she had spoken. Mouth already framing the momentous news, he changed mid-
stream.

"You'll never...manage to eat all this, Dora," he
amended lamely.

"Just try me!" she said, her eyes fixed on the plate.
"Are those lobster patties? I've never had one before.
Lady Lingdale, may I not have just one glass of cham-
pagne? I've never tried that, either."

"Certainly not, dear." The response was automatic; her
eyes were fixed over Theodora's shoulder to where their
hostess, all a-flutter, was greeting the distinguished guest,
and presenting her hastily summoned daughter. Not much
surprised, since she had not really expected to be allowed
it, Theodora applied herself to her food. Now that she was
over her nerves she found herself very hungry; she had
been unable to swallow more than bread and butter all day.

It was not until a shadow was cast over her plate that she
was aware of the tall presence of Mr. Ravensworth. Since
she had a mouthful of very flaky puff pastry at the time,
she was able to reply to his greeting with no more than an
inclination, but her eyes danced. He did not introduce the
gentleman standing beside him, though she had a vague
thought that the smooth, almost boyish face with its head

of soft brown curls was familiar. Theodora, for some reason she did not wish to examine too closely, was anxious to know Ravensworth's reaction to her appearance, and scanned his face closely. It revealed nothing.

"You are enjoying your first party, Miss Waverton?" he enquired with civility.

"Oh, yes, thank you very much! Everyone has been so kind!"

"Perhaps you will give me the honour of a dance, after supper?"

This was said with so much the air of one humouring a child that she responded, with sweet insincerity, "It is so kind of you, but I hardly think I should dare! I am accustomed to dancing with Edmund, and our steps suit so well, but on this—this *glincy* floor, I am quite nervous!"

Lady Lingdale, in the act of drinking, choked on her champagne, and was unable to speak. Mr. Ravensworth's companion, however, gave a slight smile.

"What an interesting word—glincy! I do not believe I have ever heard it before. What does it mean?"

She gave him her candid smile.

"Why, it is a Sussex word, and it means smooth, or slippery. Like ice, you know!"

"So you are from Silly Sussex! Do you often converse in the language of the natives?"

"Only sometimes, sir. I am afraid Lady Lingdale does not care for it, but it is so colourful!"

"Perhaps you would give us another example?"

Lady Lingdale's eyes were imploring, and Edmund was holding his breath. Theodora glanced up at Mr. Ravensworth, but his face betrayed no more than polite interest.

"Well, then. I might say that I am agitated when the movement of the dance goes diagonally, and if I had been allowed any of this champagne—which I have not!—I should make a disaster of it, I think. But my acquain-

tances in the Forest would put it, 'Proper vlothered, I be,
when daance goos caterwise; yif I were concarned in li-
quor I'd make a tidy avick of it, I bluv!' I put it to you, sir,
which is the more expressive?''

Lady Lingdale's moan of anguish was drowned in the
general laughter, in which the stranger joined.

"We must meet again, and you must teach me some
more of your wonderful language! My congratulations,
Lady Lingdale: an original to enliven these dull times!'' He
gave an elegant bow, and strolled away. Ravensworth went
with him, and Theodora, who had secretly hoped that he
would renew his request for a dance, was piqued, and
sought solace in food.

"Is that Rhenish Cream in that dish? Oh, good, I am
very fond of it.''

Lady Lingdale put away her handkerchief, with which
she had been dabbing her lips. "How can you think of
food, at a time like this?''

"I beg your pardon, Lady Lingdale. I know I should not
eat so much, but I am so hungry, and it is so very good!
Next time, I promise, I shall eat before coming out, so that
I may just nibble, in a ladylike way. Except that it does
seem such a waste,'' she added thoughtfully. "Edmund,
may I have an ice?''

Edmund gave a shout of laughter.

"You don't know, do you? What you've done, I
mean?''

"No, I don't. And if you mean I have some cream on my
nose, or something, I wish you would say so, Edmund,
instead of being cryptic.'' She squinted crossly down at her
person, trying to find the reason for his laughter.

Lady Lingdale found her voice.

"What Edmund means, my dear, is that you have just,
by means which I shudder to think of, assured your own
success. Did you not recognise the gentleman you were just
speaking to?''

"Mr. Ravensworth? Of course I did. I thought he wanted to dance with me, but he was just teasing, as usual, I suppose."

"Far from teasing you, he has done you the greatest service within his power. He brought his friend, Mr. Brummell, to meet you."

"Mr.—you mean, Mr. Brummell? *The* Mr. Brummell?"

"Of course! There is only one Mr. Brummell—that is, I believe he has a brother in the country, but no one takes any account of him, that I know of! Now I am gabbling, but you must put it down to relief, my dear."

"Mr. Brummell." Theodora was stunned. Now she had been told, she wondered how she had not realised. The set of his neckcloth alone should have been enough to enlighten her. "I did not know he was invited. I thought he did not attend such parties as these, unless they were given by his particular friends."

"He does not, as a rule, and that is what makes it so particularly gratifying! It is all Alexander's doing! I declare I shall never say another unkind thing about him, after this!"

"Mr. Brummell! And I talked Sussex to him!" The full enormity of what had happened was only just beginning to dawn on Theodora.

"Exactly! I must own my heart was in my mouth, for the one thing he dislikes above everything else, you know, is any hint of vulgarity. He is not at all fond of the country, or country pursuits, which makes one wonder why he and Ravensworth are such friends. But he was pleased with you! My dear, dear child, you actually made him laugh! You are made!"

"Mr. Ravensworth has been...most kind. And yet..."

"And yet what? You surely do not believe that you would have been able to attract Mr. Brummell's attention in the normal way of things, do you?"

"No, no, of course not! But Mr. Ravensworth knows only too well what I am like, I fear, and I invariably seem to behave at my worst when I am in his company. How did he know that Mr. Brummell would be pleased with me? It was more likely, surely, that he would take me in disgust, and then I would have been ruined socially."

Lady Lingdale looked at her in horror. "You don't think...?"

"I don't know what I think! All I know is, should Mr. Brummell have found me gauche, or vulgar, it would have been better that we should never have met."

Lady Lingdale was no fool. Even her partiality could not disguise the fact that Mr. Ravensworth, as a marriage prospect, outshone her Edmund as the sun outshone a tallow dip. He might not have a title, but she knew for a fact that he might have had one, had he chose, and that the simple "Mr." was in his name an honorific to conjure with. He was also, she could not deny, a very attractive man, and she did not want to risk Theodora's losing her heart—and her possible fortune—to him.

"It is a shocking thought, but I must admit that the idea cannot but cross one's mind," she allowed. "That is the trouble with Ravensworth—one never knows! Well, if that was his aim, he has been well served, and we have nothing to complain of, my dear. We shall be invited everywhere now, you will see!"

She was certainly correct. Lady Sherbury, their hostess that evening, was overwhelmingly grateful for the chance to be able to say that Mr. Brummell had graced her simple party, and passed the word around that Miss Waverton was bound to be one of the Season's successes. Invitations came so thick and fast that it was difficult to know which

ones to choose, and Theodora's letters to her mother began to read like a social directory. As a final accolade,
Lady Lingdale was delighted to receive a call from Lady
Jersey, who stayed for fifteen minutes, talked almost
without ceasing, and ended by promising vouchers for Almack's for "the little Original."

Lady Lingdale and Theodora were over the moon. Edmund was less so.

"I know it is a great honour, and all that, but it is slow
stuff," he grumbled. "I am getting very tired of all this
gadding about. I never have time to write."

"Oh, Edmund, I am so sorry! Is your leg still painful?
We do not have to go, do we, Lady Lingdale, if Edmund
does not wish it?"

"Not go, when Lady Jersey came especially to see you?
Whatever are you thinking of?" Lady Lingdale, flown
with heady triumph, was horrified. "I did not know your
leg was still hurting, Edmund."

"No, it isn't. But all these parties, it's such a bore!"

"How can you be so ridiculous, Edmund?" For once
Lady Lingdale was quite out of patience with her adored
offspring. She could not understand how he, who professed to love Theodora, could complain at spending so
much time in her company. The fact was, as Theodora had
thought from the beginning, that his passion was not really more than a passing fancy. That he should fall for the
first pretty girl he got to know was not surprising, but in
truth he was not yet ready to settle to such a life. His wings
were sprouting with a vengeance now. He wanted to travel,
to experience life, even—though it pained him to admit
that Ravensworth might have been right—to spend some
time at the university.

Theodora guessed some, if not all, of this. She sym-
pathised with his wish to lead his own life, and, if she felt
a tiny pang that her first cavalier should tire of her so

quickly, she did not allow herself to acknowledge it. Knowing that his mama would be disappointed, she did her best to humour him, while at the same time trying to prepare Lady Lingdale for the inevitable disclosure.

One thing, increasingly, was puzzling her. That Lady Lingdale should invite her, in return for helping Edmund, she had accepted as normal. Her own success was the more pleasing to her, because it gave some return for her hostess's generosity. What she could not understand was why her ladyship, knowing as she must do that her fortune was small, should be so eager to promote a marriage with her precious Edmund. When she learned that, among the court of young men who surrounded her, were one or two known fortune-hunters, she was alarmed. It was not a subject she felt able to discuss with Lady Lingdale, and Ravensworth, the only person who might, she thought, have been able to enlighten her, was keeping his distance. She told herself, crossly, that he had indeed intended to discredit her in Mr. Brummell's eyes, and was now annoyed that his plan had backfired. Deep within her she knew that such behaviour was beneath him, but she suppressed the knowledge, and fed her anger.

As she made herself ready for Almack's, on that momentous Wednesday evening, she determined that if Ravensworth should be there she would somehow find an opportunity to question him. Her gown, after much deliberation, was a daring creation of white silk georgette, with an overdress of openwork silk netting that curved over the line of the bosom and fell, clinging, to an edging of silky tassels where the V of the net finished some inches above the hem. Open at the front, the netting was edged with little pearly beads that fastened it together at the high waistline. The modiste, well satisfied with the success of her young customer, had sent it round not two days before, at a price which, though still a shock, was still too good to resist. Little shell-shaped earrings and a head-dress decorated with flowers formed of tiny sea shells completed the ensemble.

Edmund, under pressure from his mother, escorted them. It was not his first visit to the sacred portals; he would not admit that he was overawed, but even he was impressed when the doors opened, soon after their arrival, to admit the Prince Regent.

Theodora, who had just seen Mr. Ravensworth across the room, and was fixing him with what she hoped was a summoning eye, was forced, with everyone else, to stay where she was.

She had already glimpsed the Prince, at a distance, several times, but this was the first opportunity to see him near to, and she was busily storing up impressions in her mind, to write to her mother. Attracted, perhaps, by her wide-eyed stare, the Regent surged to a halt by her side. A murmur to an aide, and "May I present Miss Waverton, sir, who is newly arrived in London?"

She sank into a graceful curtsy, and he raised her with that kindly good humour that he often displayed.

"So you are the young lady from Sussex that Alvanley has told us about? It is a county I am very fond of, very fond of indeed. You know I have a little place there, by the sea. Dash me, if you wouldn't fit in there as if the place were made for you! Wouldn't she? And what hearts are you hoping to catch in those pretty nets tonight, eh?"

"If I have been lucky enough to catch your Highness's kind attention, what more could I fish—or wish—for?"

"Ha! Prettily said! Very prettily said, on my word! 'Fish for—wish for!' I must remember that!" Theodora curtsied low again, and he passed ponderously on. Theodora was at once surrounded by well-wishers, so that Mr. Ravensworth, obedient to her look, had to wait his turn. She was not displeased to see it.

"First Brummell, and now the Regent! I shall soon be able to dine out on the fact that I know you. How do you do, Cousin Amelia? I do not need to ask, of course. And my ward? Are you enjoying your first Season, Edmund?"

Edmund returned a noncommittal answer, but Lady Lingdale was disposed to be pleased with everybody, at that moment.

"Dear little Theodora! I do believe she is the talk of the town. I am positively besieged by people wanting to dance with her!"

"Then I shall not risk another set-down by requesting the pleasure," he said, maddeningly, and started to withdraw.

"Mr. Ravensworth! I owe you such a debt of gratitude, for bringing Mr. Brummell to Lady Sherbury's party, that I can refuse you nothing!" Theodora held out her hand, and he took it, raising one eyebrow.

"I was not aware that I had asked you, but I have a beautiful nature, and never bear a grudge," he murmured, leading her into the set that was just forming.

Alas for her plans. It was, as she should have realised, quite impossible to hold a private conversation during the dance, for the movements took them apart almost as soon as they came together, and, short of announcing her difficulties to the listening ears of their neighbours, she could see no way of doing it.

"I must speak to you," she hissed, as their hands met. "Privately," she added. He smiled and bowed, expressing in the act of dancing his perfect comprehension. She could only hope that he would give her the opportunity, for she could scarcely chase him into a corner.

He danced well, his hands strong on hers. Once, when the figure required him to clasp her waist, she found her eyes flying up to his, cheeks flaming. His look was hard to read. Was there, could there be, warmth in those hazel eyes? To her amazement he lifted her hand swiftly to his lips. Even through the kid of her glove she could feel the heat of that kiss, which was so quick that no one but she had noticed it. Blushing adorably, she lowered her eyes, and at the end of the dance fled back to Lady Lingdale's shelter, where he bowed, and left her.

CHAPTER EIGHT

THE EVENING at Almack's, to which Theodora had looked forward with unalloyed pleasure, was somehow flatter than she had expected. Describing, in her letter to her mother, the events that had taken place, she was glad to be able to fill the pages with a description of the Regent.

He was *very* affable, and his countenance most friendly and benign. He is certainly very large, amazingly so, in fact, but his bearing is so regal that while conversing with him I was scarcely aware of it. His waistcoat was very fine, of satin embroidered with gold, and I could not help thinking how much work it must be, to cover so large an area! Oh, dear, I hope that is not treasonable! The Prince, they say, is very sensitive about his size, and Mr. Ravensworth says that it is one of the reasons why he has fallen out with Mr. Brummell, as I believe I told you in my earlier letter.

She sat back, and reread what she had written, nibbling reflectively at the end of her pen, in lieu of her fingernails, which were now a neat almond shape, and of which she was inordinately proud. Somehow, though one was quite happy, in general, to append a list of one's dancing partners, one did not want to mention to Mama that disturbing dance with Mr. Ravensworth.

The letter was scarcely completed before Lady Lingdale was at the door, informing her that she had a message from Mr. Ravensworth.

"He invites you to drive with him, this morning! Out to Richmond Park!"

"Oh, dear!" exclaimed Theodora without thinking. "Must I really go, ma'am? I would rather not. Surely it is not proper for me to go alone with him?"

Lady Lingdale, who had come prepared to advise against the expedition should her charge show herself too eager, hesitated. After Theodora had more or less pushed Ravensworth into dancing with her the previous evening, the older woman was more than usually nervous of a romance in that direction, but Theodora's artless words set her mind at rest.

"In an open carriage, with his servant behind, it is quite allowable, I think; but I know what you mean, and I do so sympathise! Nevertheless, he is very fashionable, you know, and we must not forget that he might still set Mr. Brummell against you."

"Could he? He has always said that one of Mr. Brummell's great charms is that he is quite the reverse of changeable, and is always loyal to those he has honoured with his approbation."

"Well, maybe, but I should not like you to risk it. I dare say it will not be too bad. At least you are not frightened of him, are you, dear child? Not like my poor Edmund. Of course, Edmund was always such a sensitive boy. When I think how Ravensworth was on at me to send him away to school!"

"I thought he and Edmund had been on better terms recently? I was so glad to see it."

"So was I, but Edmund is so moody now that there is no getting any sense out of him! You have not...there has not been any little disagreement between you?" she enquired delicately.

"Not that I was aware of! I am afraid he does not always enjoy the things that we like, but that is only to be expected, after all! It would be a strange thing if a young man of his age should want to spend all his time at parties! Besides, there is his writing to consider, also. He has scarcely had time to set pen to paper since we reached London."

Lady Lingdale, who was exceedingly proud of her son's artistic skills, could not resist such a reminder. Nevertheless she was finding it increasingly difficult to understand just what her adored son did want. If Theodora was, as Lady Lingdale was convinced was the case, her rich greatuncle's heiress, then nothing could have made her ladyship happier than to see them united, for she was becoming sincerely fond of her young guest.

Edmund, given every chance to press his suit, was, however, proving a little recalcitrant, and Lady Lingdale found herself, for the first time in her life, unable to bring him to order. She was inclined, quite unfairly, to blame his change of character on the influence of his guardian, who had recently been encouraging Edmund to pursue the life of a young man about town, and had even, to her horror, taken him to Brooks'.

Theodora prepared in some trepidation for her outing, comforting herself with the undoubted fact that she had asked for the chance of private speech with Ravensworth, and also with the knowledge that she was dressed in a most fashionable outfit. The green velvet pelisse, in the military style, was topped with a neat bonnet in matching velvet, while kid half-boots of the exact same shade shod her small feet. Though the air was cold, the April sun shone brightly, and encouraged her to sport a pair of pale primrose gloves and a dashing primrose parasol. Thus armoured, she was handed with the greatest ceremony into Ravensworth's phaeton.

"It is very high up," she remarked after he had gathered the reins in his hands.

"Are you frightened? You need not be—I never overturn my phaeton on Thursdays."

"Frightened? Of course not. I was enjoying it; there is such a good view. You make the driving look so easy. May I try, or is letting others drive your horses something else you never do on Thursdays?"

"As a general rule, it is," he agreed gravely, "but, since this is the third Thursday in the month, I may make an exception. Not until we are clear of the traffic, however."

She fell silent as he negotiated a dray, and pulled up suddenly to avoid a dog. It was a beautiful day, fresh, but with a hint of summer to come, and the flower-sellers' stands were full of daffodils.

"Ah, that reminds me of home! Only there, of course, they are growing in the garden, and the orchard. I think I like them best of all there, under the apple trees."

"Would you like some? My tiger can fetch them."

"Oh, no, thank you. They would die before I could get them home, and they are not very practical to hold. The stems dribble, you know."

"Do they? How unpleasant. You have quite disillusioned me. I shall never be able to look a daffodil in the face again." She smiled. "You wanted to speak to me, Miss Waverton. Have you changed your mind?"

She glanced involuntarily at his servant, seated up behind them in his livery.

"You need not worry about my tiger. He is very discreet, and has been with me for years. Besides, he is only interested in the horses; he thinks people are very dull."

She found that her hands were gripped together and loosened her clasp, smoothing the soft yellow kid.

"It is about my money, Mr. Ravensworth."

"Your money? Run yourself to a standstill, have you? I'm not surprised. That gown you had on last night— Neptune's dream, or whatever it was—must have cost a pretty penny, besides the other creations I keep seeing you in."

"It's not that! My evening gown was supplied at a much reduced cost, let me tell you, because Madame thinks I am a good advertisement for her. I have tried very hard not to be extravagant."

"I was not criticising! You looked charming last night, and every other time I have seen you, come to that."

"You have only seen me twice," she said, unwisely.

"You mean, *you* have only seen *me* twice," he corrected her. "I have been keeping an eye on you, Miss Waverton."

"Why?" she asked bluntly.

"Would you believe me if I said my motives were of the most benevolent? I felt, in some sort, responsible for you. I wanted to be sure that you were enjoying yourself."

"And not ensnaring your ward?"

"That too, of course. I told your mother, some while ago, that, since you were his equal by birth and breeding, I would have no objection to the match, if he wanted it. Now, however, I have changed my mind."

"It is nothing to do with you!"

"On the contrary, it is everything to do with me. I tell you here and now, Miss Waverton, that I will do my utmost to see that you do not marry Edmund."

"And I tell you here and now, Mr. Ravensworth, that your utmost can never be enough!" In a towering rage, and completely ignoring the fact that she had not the least wish to marry Edmund, she would have walked up the aisle with him then and there if it had been possible. Tears of rage filled her eyes, and she turned her face away from her escort. They ran down her face, cold against her cheeks, and she ignored them stalwartly. She had made no sound, but his hand came out and placed a large, freshly laundered white handkerchief in her lap. For a few minutes she ignored it, but in the end was forced to avail herself of it, drying her cheeks and giving her nose a defiant blow. It smelled of Russia leather, and against her will she was carried back to their first meeting in the Forest.

"That is better. You must believe that I have no wish to distress you, Theodora."

"I do not believe I made you free of my name, sir," she said shakily.

"Miss Waverton, then. If you are worried about money, you may always apply to me."

She had by now completely forgotten the beginning of their conversation. "Money? I am not worried about money!"

"You are quite sure? You need not be embarrassed to tell me, you know. If there are debts you are unable to meet..."

"I don't know what you are talking about! I have no debts! I don't understand you, Mr. Ravensworth. First you say you will never allow me to marry Edmund, and then you offer to pay my non-existent debts! Do you think I have been gambling like my father? Is that why you have been keeping an eye on me?"

"Of course not. And I think you know that very well, Miss Waverton, if you were not so determined to take offence at everything I say!"

"It is offensive to me when you say you will not allow me to marry Edmund."

"If I thought that was what you really wanted, I would never stand in your way. As it is, my reasons for refusing it are such that I prefer, at present, not to mention them. You may consider this cowardly, if you will, but I assure you that the other thing I never do on Thursdays is to lay myself open to ridicule.''

She stole a glance at him. His face was as unrevealing as ever, but a small frown creased his forehead between those dark brows.

"I do not understand you," she said in a small voice.

"I am well aware of that. Which is why, my dear Miss Waverton, I do not wish to continue the conversation. If you are not in difficulties over money, why did you want to speak to me on the subject?"

The sudden change of tack took Theodora aback, but distracted her mind, as he had intended, from his cryptic words.

"My difficulty, Mr. Ravensworth, is that there seems to be some rumour afoot that I am an heiress! You must know as well as I do that I have no fortune, or at least only a very modest one, from my father. I am not ashamed of the fact, but I do not want to be courted under false pretences."

"What makes you think that you are?"

"If your eye has been upon me, as you say it has, it cannot have escaped your notice that among those who regularly solicit my company for dances are at least two men who are well known to be hanging out for a fortune. Moreover, though I should not perhaps impute such motives to one who has been so kind to me, I am surprised to find that Lady Lingdale seems to be using every means within her power to encourage Edmund to offer for me! Knowing her as you must do, does that not seem strange to you? Gratitude to me for my service to her son is one thing, but I cannot believe that gratitude alone would be enough to make her forgo all her hopes and wishes for him to make a great match."

Ravensworth looked grave.

"I fear I am not wholly innocent in this matter. It will come as no surprise to you, I suppose, that my cousin was at first very concerned to find that Edmund was casting his eyes in your direction. She asked my advice. I must admit that at the time I thought that he was too young to be forming a serious attachment, and that this calf-love would soon be outgrown."

"That is not very flattering to me."

"It has nothing to do with it. Brought up as he has been, deprived of company of his own age, I would have been surprised if he had not fancied himself in love with a very pretty girl, whom he had met in such very romantic circumstances. It was only to be expected. Nor is it surprising that he should subsequently find that such sudden passions, based more on propinquity than on any real appreciation of the young lady's undoubted gifts, should fade away later on."

"You forget, I think, that I was also brought up in an equally solitary manner. Did you not expect equally that I would fall in love with him? He is very handsome, after all."

"Oh, a paragon, I grant you. Can it be, Miss Waverton, that I may give you credit for more sense than he has? In any case, I felt that Lady Lingdale need have few apprehensions for her son, but, knowing something of your situation, I felt that you deserved the chance of spreading your wings. I therefore encouraged Cousin Amelia, as best I could, to see you in a rosy light."

"You did not tell her that I was an heiress? How could you, when you must have known that the reverse is true! You surely did not think that you did me any service, to spread false rumours about my fortune?"

"On the contrary. I told her exactly what your situation is. But I also informed her of what is true, which is that you and your mother are the only living relatives of Jonas Bellerby."

"Jonas Bellerby? Who is he, pray? I have no knowledge of any such man."

"Has your mother never spoken to you of him? He is her uncle."

"Him? I never knew his name. But he and Mama have not communicated since I was a small child! If you know anything of my history, you will perhaps be aware that this Mr. Bellerby encouraged—nay, forced—my mother, at a scandalously young age, into marriage with my father, to further his own political ends. It is true that for a while he made my mother an allowance—which is why, incidentally, she keeps the name of Allendale, since it was one of the conditions—but he did so very unwillingly. I believe his only motive was fear of scandal. As soon as my mother was able to support herself by her writing, she refused to accept his allowance."

"I was not unaware of most of this, though I did not know that he had ever made any allowance at all. It is well known that he lives the life of a recluse, almost of a miser, and has no family that he acknowledges. It is also known that he has strong feelings about inheritance—that it should whenever possible stay within the family. This is a matter of common knowledge. I merely pointed out to Amelia your position, as one of his only two living relatives. The inferences she drew for herself."

"He is very rich, I suppose?"

"Immensely so."

Theodora fell silent. However sensible one might be, it was nevertheless hurtful to discover that the warmth of affection, that one had supposed animated by oneself, was in fact no more than a love of one's presumed fortune.

"It is understandable, I suppose, that Lady Lingdale should want Edmund to marry someone wealthy." Despite her efforts, her tone was sad.

"You must not think that you are courted only for your fortune. Edmund, at least, knows nothing of this, and I am fairly sure that no one else is aware of the relationship. Bellerby is a very old man, and has lived out of the way so long that few people realise he is still alive."

"Yet someone must have put the word about, somehow. I am certainly regarded as an heiress," she said bitterly.

"I am afraid that, like you, most people are unable to believe that my cousin would countenance a match between Edmund and a girl of little fortune, however beautiful and amiable. I perceive I was at fault ever to have mentioned it to her. I took good care, at the time, to point out that I had no idea of your actually being likely to inherit; I merely pointed out the relationship. I hope you will accept my apologies."

She had never heard him speak in so quiet a tone, his looks and voice almost supplicating. For once, though he had in fact done something perhaps worse than the other slights and annoyances that had so annoyed her, she could not find it in her to upbraid him. For one thing, how much she had enjoyed her visit to London, which would never have taken place without his interference.

"I forgive you, of course," she said sighing, "but what is to be done?"

"You are very forbearing. I do not think that there is anything, at this time, that you may do. You are not likely, I suppose, to wish to marry either of your devoted fortune-hunters? In fact, though you may not know it, you have done much in the past few weeks to make you in truth what they think you are already."

"How so?"

"My dear girl, by your success! After money, which is his God, Jonas Bellerby worships Society! Not that he has ever, in truth, been a part of it—he has little to make him popular, except his money, and with that he has always been so clutch-fisted that he will not even spend it to buy himself some acclaim. But he loves, or used to love, to mingle with the great. To have his young relative lauded and fêted by the ton will fill him with delight."

"I am not so great a success as all that," she said.

"You think not? I must tell you that Brummell has spoken very highly of you to the Duchess of York—you know they are the best of friends—and she means to ask you to visit Oatlands quite soon. She may be a little eccentric, but I know of few people whose opinions are so valued. The Regent has been seen to compliment you, and his sister-in-law invites you to visit; it is difficult to see how you could be more successful, unless you intend to supplant the Royal favourites, and I am afraid you are too young and slim for Prinny—he prefers a nice, plump grandmother!"

Theodora ignored his levity.

"Are you serious? About the Duchess of York, I mean? She does not mix in Society a great deal, does she?"

"No, I really think she prefers animals to people. You know that she keeps an enormous number of dogs, as well as monkeys, ostriches, kangaroos, and I don't know what else!"

"How very singular! Not but what I prefer the company of my dear Jason to many people I know."

"Such as myself? Do not trouble to deny it; I am well aware of the fact! You must admit, however, that, if I have occasionally terrorised my ward, I have never actually attempted any physical assault on him!"

"That was all in fun! You must have seen that Jason was only showing his affection!"

"Then I sincerely hope he never decides that he is fond of me."

"I don't know... sometimes he likes the most surprising people."

"Stop trying to score points off me, and notice that we have now reached the Park. We will pause in our delightful conversation, so that you may comment inanely upon the beauties of the scene. I will then give a gratified smirk, as if I had created the whole for your especial benefit, and we may be rational again."

Theodora's ready sense of fun never deserted her for long.

"How silly you are! I *must* remark that it is beautiful, you know, for how could I do otherwise? And are those deer I see over there? How wonderful; I have not seen a deer since I left Sussex."

"Do not, I implore you, become all rustic, and treat me to a display of dialect!"

"Oh, no, I keep that for my most particular friends," she responded sweetly. "Please tell me about this invitation to Oatlands Park; it sounds rather alarming. Will the Duke be there, do you think? I have never seen him, but he sounds fearsome."

"York? Fearsome? Oh, no. It is true that he is rather loud, and given to cursing, but never unpleasantly. He is very affectionate and jovial, generous to a fault, and always stands by his word. Would that one might say the same about our future Monarch! There, now I have placed myself utterly in your hands—if you should repeat that remark injudiciously, I should never be forgiven. I have no dislike for the Regent, but I have no great respect for him either. His brother is worth two of him. The pity of it is that the Yorks are childless."

"Perhaps that is why she is so fond of her pets. I have seen it before, in the village. It is a need for something to love."

"Very likely. Anyway, to answer your question, the Duke is only at Oatlands at weekends. I should tell you that your invitation is a great honour; in general, Princess Fred prefers gentlemen. I am sure you will enjoy the visit; if nothing else, the grotto is sure to please you."

"How shall I get there? Will you take me?" she asked rather shyly. To be invited to visit, by Royalty, was so outside her scope of experience that she was a little daunted by the prospect, honour though it was.

"My carriage is certainly at your disposal, if Lady Lingdale cannot spare hers. You will probably be invited to spend two or three days there, though it is not too far for a visit of only one day. The Duchess prefers to have a chance to get to know her guests in this way. If it is the weekend, there will probably be a crowd, and the Duke may well be there also. During the week there are fewer people."

"I hope it will be during the week, then. It sounds less frightening."

"Then I will try to put in a suggestion to that effect—or perhaps Brummell will. He is very taken with you. Of course, Lady Lingdale will be delighted with you, and Mr. Bellerby also, should he come to hear of it. He probably will—he lives not far from Oatlands, you know."

"I want to please Lady Lingdale, of course—how should I not, when she has been so good to me?—but, as for Mr. Bellerby, I do not give a snap of my fingers for his opinion, good or bad."

"You do not need to tell me that. Miss Waverton, you are agitating yourself to no avail. Will you not, just for this once, take my advice, and put all this from your mind?

Enjoy your visit to Oatlands, and let everything else take its course?''

"Let be how 'twill, in fact.''

He groaned.

"If you must so express yourself, yes. Let be how 'twill.''

For once, Theodora thought she had managed to have the last word. This gave her considerable pleasure, and enabled her to converse, in a civilised fashion, during their journey back to Mount Street. Mr. Ravensworth proved surprisingly knowledgeable about books and poetry. Theodora was astonished to find him so well-read, and did not hesitate to inform him so.

"Do I appear to be such a yahoo? I had no idea.''

She had the grace to blush.

"Not a yahoo, precisely, but I know what a keen sportsman you are.''

"The one does not preclude the other, you know! I do not think my friend Brummell would have much time for me were I only interested in hunting, and shooting, and driving, for you must know he cares nothing for such things! In fact, my conceit leads me to inform you that I have actually been able to make a contribution to his celebrated book. Normally, I should hesitate to boast, but your opinion of me is so low that I am sure I cannot make it any worse.''

Theodora was too interested to pick up this blatant piece of teasing.

"His book? What is that?''

"You have not heard of it? Brummell keeps a book, specially bound in blue velvet, in which he inscribes verses written for him by his friends—if they are good enough, that is! I can assure you, it is a great honour to appear in it! Princess Fred has done so several times, of course, and the late Duchess of Devonshire. I suppose you might say it is his commonplace book, though he would very much resent such an appellation.''

"How I should love to see it!''

"Well, if he should be at Oatlands when you are there, you must make sure to ask him, for nothing pleases him more than displaying it. He is very proud of it, and the great names to be found therein!''

He spoke with the cheerful disparagement of one who sees, but almost loves, the foibles of his friend. Theodora, who had never seen him like this before, was interested.

"What kind of man is he—Mr. Brummell? He has never married, has he?''

"No, nor do I think he will. Not that he is not in every respect a proper man; only, that his life is so full, so happy, that he needs no one else in it. There is a great deal of self-love, but it is so ironical, so candidly displayed, that one cannot dislike it in him. He is very much cleverer than most people give him credit for; indeed, the only thing I truly deplore in him is his propensity for gaming.''

"You do not gamble yourself, Mr. Ravensworth?''

They were approaching Mount Street. Theodora spoke indignantly; she knew very well that he did. He looked down at her.

"I do, but neither as often, nor as recklessly. And, at the risk of boasting again, I can afford to do so, which Brummell cannot. Now, I suppose, you will devastate me with some earthy Sussex phrase?''

"Not at all. I must thank you, Mr. Ravensworth, for a most enjoyable drive.''

"Liar,'' he returned equably. "What you mean is, you do not wish me to accompany you into the house.''

"How you do take one up,'' she sighed. "What did you expect me to say?''

He looked at her, suddenly serious.

"To me, Theodora, you may always say what is in your heart."

She blushed adorably, looked away, and tumbled out of the phaeton almost as soon as he had pulled up, so that his servant had to run to assist her down. Ravensworth said no more, but watched her up the steps. As soon as the door was opened he gave a careless nod, and drove away.

"Well!" said Theodora to herself. "Well, really!" She then found herself unwilling to continue this soliloquy, for fear of what she might hear, so composed her face and mind in preparation for Lady Lingdale's inevitable enquiries.

CHAPTER NINE

THE INVITATION, when it arrived, was couched in the most friendly and informal terms. Theodora was assured that the gathering, during her two nights' visit, would be composed only of a few of the Duchess's particular friends, most of them gentlemen. The proprieties, however, were observed by the presence—apart from the Duchess herself—of her lady of the bedchamber, Lady Anne Culling Smith, and Lady Anne's three daughters.

Nevertheless, it was with some trepidation that Theodora, accompanied by her maid, stepped into Mr. Ravensworth's carriage. She did not know whether to be relieved or disappointed to learn that he did not intend to travel with her. On the one hand she had no wish to have another disagreement with him like the last, when she was about to make so grand a visit, but on the other, a familiar face would have been welcome, with so much grandeur in prospect.

She need not have worried. At weekends, the Duchess played hostess to gatherings, not only of the wealthy and the well-born, but also of intellectuals and wits, for she delighted in collecting around her people of high spirits and good conversation. Much though Theodora would have enjoyed meeting some of them, on balance she felt that she was quite unable to contemplate sustaining such an honour, and the small gathering she would be joining would be quite alarming enough. She wrote that afternoon to her mother.

So here I am, actually at Oatlands, I have not seen very much of the Duchess yet, although she greeted me very pleasantly at luncheon, soon after I arrived. She is small, like me, and her feet are the tiniest I ever saw! She was much concerned about one of her pets, a dog, which was ill, and could think of nothing else. It seems likely that a new burial will shortly be taking place by the grotto, which I have not yet seen, but hope to shortly. Lady Anne Fitzroy—Lady Anne Culling Smith's daughter by a previous marriage—has been kind enough to offer to show it to me later. How I wonder at finding myself in so elevated a company! You will be interested, I know, to hear that Mr. Lewis, the author of *Ambrosio*, or *The Monk*, is here. He is such an oddity! Little, and with protruding eyes just like the Vicarage dog! Mr. Ravensworth is very much at home here, and I believe Mr. Brummell is expected some time this afternoon. Did you ever expect to see your little chick flying with such a flock of eagles? It is time to visit the grotto, and I must not keep Lady Anne waiting. I will write again later, dearest Mama, and try to remember everything I see!

"You travelled down in Mr. Ravensworth's carriage, did you not?" quizzed Lady Anne, as they walked through the gardens. "Is he related to you?"

"No, not at all," replied Theodora firmly. "He is related to Lady Lingdale, who has been so very kind in inviting me to stay with her, and he is her son's guardian. I suppose, as her guest, he extends such courtesies to me."

"Then you are not connected with the family at all? Forgive me, I do not wish to pry, but it is rare for the Duchess to invite a young lady, for to be honest she prefers gentlemen. Not that I mean that in any derogatory way, of course! Mr. Brummell is one of her greatest friends, and is always visiting, and Mr. Ravensworth is often invited, as one of Mr. Brummell's set. He is very handsome, don't you think?'' Theodora returned an evasive answer. ''I see you will not be drawn on that subject! I will not tease you by pursuing it.''

They reached the grotto, which consisted of no less than three rooms, decorated with sea shells and stalactites. In front of it was an ornamental basin, surrounded by the graves of many departed pets, and it looked out over a pretty prospect of pond and woodland.

''How charming it is! I have never seen anything like it!'' exclaimed Theodora. ''But then, of course, I have never been anywhere before, until this year. I have passed the whole of my life in the Ashdown Forest, in Sussex.''

''That must be very beautiful?''

''Oh, yes! I love it above everything. But this is so elegant, so delightful! These shells, they are real? I have never seen the sea, you know.''

''Yes, they are real, though not the stalactites, of course. This is the Duchess's favourite place—she frequently dines and breakfasts here, during the week, and at weekends the Duke plays whist here.''

''Forgive me, but . . . the Duke and Duchess are very much apart?''

''Yes, I do not mean that they do not get on, though I believe that when they were first married the Duchess was much neglected. Now they are good friends, and we all go on very merrily together.''

''I wish I were better at sketching,'' said Theodora wistfully. ''I would like to show my mama how it all is, and mere words are never enough.''

''She does not accompany you to London?''

''No. She thought it was better not.'' Lady Anne forebore to question, but Theodora lifted her chin and answered her look with her usual forthright manner. ''My mother has lived apart from my father since before I was born. He is dead now, but she thinks that she might still not be acceptable to the high sticklers of Society.''

"She may be right. Here, of course, the Duchess would not think of minding it—but then, her own parents were divorced.''

"What is permissible in a Princess of Prussia might not be so acceptable in plain Lady Waverton,'' said Theodora bluntly.

"I am afraid that is true. It is the way of the world, I suppose.''

"You must not think that I am ashamed of her,'' asserted Theodora with some belligerence.

"Of course not!''

"Do not allow yourself to be intimidated by Miss Waverton, Lady Anne,'' said a lazy voice behind them, "I annoyed her only the other day, and she had me quaking in my boots!''

They both turned. Mr. Ravensworth's approach over the grass had been unintentionally silent. Now he stood before them, clad with careless elegance, towering over both of them in his gleaming, tasselled hessians. Anything less inclined to quake would have been hard to imagine, and Theodora had to suppress the smile that she saw so openly on Lady Anne's face.

Courteously he offered an arm to each of the ladies. Lady Anne did not hesitate, and Theodora found herself unable to refuse the support, though she would have preferred to. His arm was strongly muscular under the dark green sleeve of his coat, and she kept the touch of her fingers as light as she could.

"I hope your journey down was comfortable?'' he asked her.

"Yes, thank you, sir.''

"And you have met Princess Fred?''

"Her Highness has been very kind, and welcoming," she answered repressively, rather alarmed by his lack of respect.

"You need not mind! All the Duchess's friends call her that. By the by, Brummell is here, also. He arrived just before I did, so you will see him at dinner, if not before."

"I am so glad! Mr. Brummell is a delightful acquaintance, and never teases me, or tells me what I may or may not do!"

"Meaning that I do? Well, maybe. Miss Waverton is very severe with me, Lady Anne. I trust you will treat me with proper sympathy?"

"I must decline to come between the crossfire! Such wrangling presupposes an old friendship, and I should not like to spoil your pleasure!"

As Theodora went upstairs to change for dinner, she realised with a little shock that what Lady Anne had said was, in part, true. There was a pleasure in the give and take of argument between Ravensworth and herself. However much he might annoy her, he was never boring, and his quick responses stimulated her own mind as flint and steel drew sparks from one another.

It was with some relief that she had learned that she was not expected to dress in formal Court clothes. Princess Fred might be sister-in-law to the Regent, and her husband next in line to the throne after him, but here in her country home she preferred simplicity and informality. An evening gown of white silk crêpe, with an embroidered border in the Greek key design, was quite fine enough, with Mama's pearls and an elegantly draped scarf edged with the same pattern to complete the ensemble. Her hair, brushed by Mary's loving hands, glowed like a newly opened horse chestnut, and was arranged in the simple style that Lady Lingdale's hairdresser had devised for her.

Dinner was a cheerful affair, much enlivened by Brummell, who was at his best in such company. Encouraged by his gentle teasing, Theodora was emboldened to amuse her hostess by teaching her some words of Sussex origin, with which she seemed much taken. "So that thick, heavy mud I remember so disastrously clearly from your Sussex roads—you call that 'stodge'?" she enquired. "It is wonderfully apt—just the sound one's foot makes when entering or leaving it!"

"Yes, madam. Stodge, or sometimes we say the road is stoachy, also."

"Stoachy? That is even better! You must have a great deal of mud, to have so many words to describe it."

"I am afraid the nature of our soil makes that inevitable, madam. Then, of course, it gets on our feet, and is spannelled all over the floor."

The Duchess thought. "I know! As a spaniel's long coat picks up the dirt, and brings it in!"

"Just so; you have it exactly."

The Duchess was much pleased, committing the words to memory to mystify the Duke when he should next appear. Brummell, meanwhile, was being rallied on his appetite.

"Bread and cheese! That's what he lives on, you know, just bread and cheese!" Ravensworth asserted. "It is a wonder he survives, but then, of course, he never does anything strenuous."

"Come now! You would not wish me to appear all spattered with mud, and glowing with perspiration, as you hunting men do!" Looking at the perfection of his snowy linen, and black coat of Bath superfine, Theodora had to agree that the idea was unthinkable.

"You do not care for hunting, then, Mr. Brummell?" she enquired shyly.

"Oh, yes! I frequently go hunting! Only, I do not care to follow too far, so I generally take myself off to the nearest farmhouse, to sample the cheeses. I consider myself to be an expert on the subject, and British cheese, you know, is the best in the world!"

A general laugh followed this assertion.

"But you eat other things, do you not, my friend?" asked the Duchess, with a sly look at his plate, which was loaded with venison.

"My dear Duchess, at your table I eat everything! Except vegetables, of course," he added, in tones of loathing.

"Vegetables? It is true that I have never seen you partake of them."

"I am afraid I cannot find them a suitable mode of nourishment for a man of sensibility," he sighed. "Some, perhaps, but never the *green* varieties!" He gave a shudder. "So like fodder! One might as well go out and graze on the lawn!"

"And have you never eaten them?"

Brummell pondered deeply.

"Yes, madam, I once ate a pea," he admitted, with deep regret but the air of one willing to make a clean breast of past misdeeds. There was a shout of laughter from the company, and Theodora, watching his slight smile and glowing eyes, enjoyed the effrontery of his affectation, which was half serious and half, she was sure, in self-mockery.

After dinner the ladies were left alone for only a short time. The Duchess, whose concern for her ailing dog had led her to go and see it as soon as she withdrew from the table, re-entered the room where Theodora sat with Lady Anne Fitzroy, that lady's sisters, and her mother. Scarcely had the Duchess motioned them to resume their seats, when a footman entered and murmured in her ear. Her eyes strayed to Theodora, who was looking at a book of prints with Lady Anne, and before the girl was properly aware of it the servant was bowing to her, and offering a letter on a small silver tray. Theodora's eyes flew to her hostess, who nodded genially.

"A letter from a relative of yours, which has just been brought over," she said kindly. "Please do not hesitate to look it over."

"Thank you, madam, but I...I have no relative but my mother, and this is not her writing," said Theodora, with dread in her heart.

"Then you must certainly open it at once."

Theodora did so with shaking fingers. The unfamiliar hand was hard to read, and so much did she fear to learn some ill tidings of her mother that at first the words, puzzled over one by one, made no sense. At last she realised that there was no mention of illness or worse, took a grip on herself, and returned to the start of the missive. It began without preamble.

If you are the daughter of the late Sir George Waverton, and his wife, then you may or may not be aware that I am your grand-uncle, or your step-grand-uncle, to be more precise. I have learned with pleasure that my youthful relative has redeemed her mother's faults by making a place for herself in Society, to the extent of being honoured by an invitation to the Royal household at Oatlands. As a near neighbour, though not an acquaintance, of the Duchess, I take this opportunity to say that I would like to make your acquaintance. I shall be at home tomorrow, as indeed I am every day, and I will expect your visit between the hours of ten and twelve.

There were no closing courtesies, merely the signature, coldly precise, of Jonas Bellerby.

Theodora raised troubled eyes to find that the other five ladies were watching her. She had no idea how the changing feelings had washed over her expressive face. She was still very pale.

"It is not bad news, I hope?" asked the Duchess kindly.

"Oh, no, madam. That is ... no."

"Your mother has suffered no illness, or accident?"

"No, no, madam. The letter has nothing to do with my mother."

She looked troubled, unconsciously folding and unfolding the letter in her hands, before laying it aside with a motion of disgust, as one who had handled something unclean.

The Duchess looked concerned.

"I hope it was not delivered to you under false pretences, then. The man said quite clearly that it was from your close relative, and I understand from Lady Anne that you and your mother are alone in the world?"

Theodora saw that she must tell the whole, or give offence.

"Forgive me, madam. I am afraid I am a little...overset. The letter is from someone I have never met, whose existence I have only recently learned of, and never expected to hear from. He is my mother's uncle, or rather step-uncle, as he was my grandfather's stepbrother. He was my mother's guardian in her childhood."

"And you have never met him? Or heard of him, until recently?"

"No, madam. My mother displeased him, and he cast her off. My mother never spoke of him until a short while ago, when she was telling me her history." She lifted her chin defiantly. "I do not know whether my mother's sad past is known to you, madam, but I must assure you that she is the best mother in the world to me, and I trust her word above anyone's."

Princess Fred chose to be amused.

"You need not defend her to me, my dear! I am sure she is all that you say. And this uncle—what is his name?"

"Jonas Bellerby, madam."

"Jonas Bellerby? I have heard of him, have I not? He lives not far from here, but is a great recluse, and never goes anywhere."

"I do not know anything about him."

"I have heard of him also, madam," put in Lady Anne Culling Smith. "He is a recluse, as you say, and reputed to be a very rich one, also."

"Indeed! And what does he want, this rich, miserly uncle?" The Duchess held out her hand, and rather unwillingly Theodora put the letter, now very creased, into it. "So he wants to see you? To be sure he does not express himself with much affection, but then, he has never met you. I think, my dear, that you should go."

"But madam . . ."

Theodora's objection was not heeded.

"It would be foolish to ignore him. If he is half as rich as they say, you cannot afford to antagonise him. Whatever occurred between him and your mother, it was a long time ago, and who knows? He may wish to make reparation, if he has done harm. I will order a chaise to take you, so you need not worry how you will get there, and it will show him that you are a valued guest. That will not do you any harm, you may be sure!"

The generosity of Royalty being tantamount to an order, Theodora swallowed her protests, and gave thanks with as much sincerity as she could call up. The matter was considered closed and, as they were almost immediately joined by the gentlemen, Theodora was able to shrink into the background for the rest of the evening.

The Duchess and her ladies, understanding that she had received a severe shock, and guessing some of her feelings of apprehension about the forthcoming visit, allowed her to remain quiet, and she hardly noticed anything about the rest of the evening. There was much talk and laughter, and she felt isolated in her bubble of unhappiness. She would have given anything to flee to her room, but it was of course unthinkable that she should withdraw before the Duchess.

"You are unwontedly silent, Miss Waverton." Unperceived, Mr. Ravensworth had made his way to the shadowed corner where she had hoped to evade notice. Suddenly, as she looked at him, it seemed to her that he was the author of all her ills. Had it not been for him, she would not have been at Oatlands at all, and wretched Mr. Bellerby would never have heard of her. She looked at him with intense dislike.

"I have nothing to say, Mr. Ravensworth. Particularly to you!"

He raised an eyebrow.

"What can I possibly have done to merit such vehemence?" To her own unspeakable annoyance, Theodora's eyes filled with tears. She turned away, but not before he had seen them. "My dear child, what has occurred to upset you like this?" The gentleness in his voice, which she had never heard before, completed her undoing, and she hiccuped on a sob, fishing distractedly in her reticule for a handkerchief. Before she could find it, his own was pressed into her hand, and once again she was obliged to accept the use of his discreetly scented linen, drying her eyes as unobtrusively as she could, and dabbing at her nose.

"Theodora! You have not allowed anything I might have said, or done, to upset you? The very last thing in the world that I want is for you to be unhappy." She shook her head, unable to speak, and finding within herself a base longing to subside on to that broad chest, and cry out her fear and dismay. The thought of his arms round her, protecting her from the world, was suddenly a thing to be longed for, and even the possibility that such an embrace might lead to such a one as he had imposed on her before held no terrors for her, but only a *frisson* of excitement.

Fighting this thought, which was in any case more than impossible in such company, she pulled from her reticule her great-uncle's letter, and handed it to him.

He turned towards the light, considerately shielding her from view with his broad back, and scanned the page, while she breathed slowly and carefully, swallowed the lump in her throat, and discreetly fanned her hot eyes.

"I see. No wonder you are upset, and I do not altogether blame you for being angry with me. I can assure you that I had no hand in this invitation, however. Will you go?"

"The Duchess asked to see the letter. She has kindly offered me the use of a chaise," she said huskily.

"Yes. Well, there's no choice in it, then. Do you want me to come with you?"

"No, thank you. It is better if I go alone."

"Very well. Do not allow him to upset you. He has no claim on you, no power over you. Your situation as the guest of the Princess makes you safe from anything he might do, I think."

She was grateful to him, an unaccustomed feeling, and when at last the company broke up for the night she said good-night to him with a shy smile that he had never seen before.

Defiantly, the following morning she dressed herself in her best-figured muslin gown, and wore the green velvet pelisse and bonnet she had put on to drive with Ravensworth. It was a dismal morning, heavily overcast and raining intermittently, and she was glad of the warmth of the velvet. May might soon be arriving, but the weather that day seemed to have reverted to that of March. The drive seemed long, and Theodora did not know whether she wished it would continue forever, or finish so that she could get the visit over with. When at last the chaise pulled into an overgrown, heavily weeded drive she was shivering with a mixture of cold and tension.

The house was large, gloomy, and appeared to be almost completely deserted. Waiting in the chaise while the servant hammered on the door, Theodora eyed the dirty windows, the green-stained brickwork where broken guttering had allowed several years' worth of rain to trickle down the walls, and the cold, smokeless chimneys with misgiving, tempered with rising hope. Maybe he was not here, and it was all a mistake!

She was about to call the servant back, and tell him to return to Oatlands, when the heavy door creaked ponderously open, and an elderly manservant put his head through the gap, like a newly wakened tortoise coming out of his shell in the spring. The servant returned, and handed her down, and she trod up the stone steps, slippery with moss and algae, and was admitted.

The house was cold, but stuffy. Many of the windows were shuttered, and in the Stygian gloom she could make out little, but this was probably just as well, judging by the black cobwebs whose movement, in the cold draught of her passing, caught her eye. Gathering her skirts fastidiously around her, she followed her speechless, wheezing guide until at last he stood back to allow her to enter a room. It was scarcely better lit than the others, for, though the shutters were open, the windows were so overgrown with ivy and creepers that little of the grey daylight could enter. No fire burned in the wide grate, by which a huge winged chair was set. In the chair, well wrapped against the cold, was the man she had come to visit.

His face was yellow and withered beneath the old-fashioned wig, the hand that gestured her nearer wrinkled, and none too clean, but the eyes were still startlingly bright. She drew nearer, standing before him, but when he waved her peremptorily to a chair in front of him she looked at it, and remained standing.

"Don't tower over me like that, girl! Where are your manners? Sit down!" The voice was thin but held the remains of power. She was momentarily diverted by the thought of herself, diminutive as she was, towering over anyone, and was enabled to dust the chair with her handkerchief before risking her expensive velvet to its seat. The handkerchief was black.

"Fussy, eh? Not good enough, I suppose, after your grand friends?" She made no reply, but sat waiting with what composure she could muster. "Not going to speak to me, then? I suppose you are poor Maria's child? You don't have much look of her."

"No one else would have any reason to be here," she pointed out, "and I came in the Duchess's chaise. Unwillingly."

He gave a crack of laughter, that turned into a cough.

"You're a bold one, aren't you?" he said with some approval, when the paroxysm had subsided. "There's many that would like to set themselves where you are, dirt or no dirt. So you didn't want to visit your poor old uncle, then?"

"No," she said baldly. "I cannot think why you have asked me."

"You're my only living relative," he pointed out, "except for Maria, and she don't count."

Theodora hid her rising anger, and remained silent.

"I'm a rich man, you know," the horrid voice continued, slicing through the silence of the dead house like a butcher's knife into cold flesh. "Richer than they know. Richer than that Ravensworth you've been setting your cap at."

"I have *not!*" She could not remain silent at that.

"Don't fire up at me, girl! I don't mind if you have! He may not have a title, but he's a man of power, of influence. I could give my approval to him."

"I am sure he would be gratified," she said icily, striving for a return to aplomb. "Your approval or disapproval means nothing to me."

"Not if it brings my fortune with it? I'm an old man, my dear. A rich old man. I could leave it all to you, if you marry to please me."

She jumped to her feet. "To please you? I'd sooner stay single all my days!"

"So you may say, so you may say. But would you really turn it down, all that fortune of mine? Think what you could do with it. Think of the clothes, the jewels, the fine houses you could have. Think of your mother, my girl. What is to become of her when she grows old, can't write those little stories and stuff any more? You wouldn't leave her to starve, would you?"

"Rather than take a penny of yours, I would starve with her," she stated in fury. He laughed.

"A girl of spirit! I like to see it! Well, the choice is yours. There is five hundred pounds, in this purse, as an earnest of my intentions. You have only to ask for it. Say, 'Uncle, I will be a dutiful niece,' and it's yours!" He shook a leather purse, which chinked dully and seemed almost beyond the strength of his aged hand. Theodora put her hands behind her back, and he laid the purse in his lap, stroking it as if it were a pet cat, so that the gold rustled and whispered together. "That's all there is to it. You have only to ask."

"I will never ask! Never!"

His cold voice followed her as she ran from the room, blindly fleeing down dim passages as though he were running, nightmare-like, behind her.

"A fortune, my dear. You only have to ask..."

More by luck than anything else she reached the door she had come in by. Tugging it open—stiff on unused hinges—she breathed the damp, rain-filled air as if it were the sweetest waft of rose-scented June. The dirty handkerchief was still in her hand, and she flung it from her in disgust as she squeezed through the gap, and, regardless of the servants' surprise, jumped into the chaise without waiting for their assistance. Drawing his own conclusions, the driver climbed into his seat and whipped up the horses. Theodora sank back against the cushions and closed her eyes.

CHAPTER TEN

BY CONCENTRATING fiercely on her anger, Theodora managed to suppress any tears during her journey back to Oatlands. Unthinkable to arrive there with watery eyes and reddened nose! By good fortune she achieved her bedroom without encountering anyone but servants, and was there able to lock herself away and indulge in the luxury of a hearty burst of tears. After that she washed her face, changed her gown, and resolved to put the nasty old man out of her mind, and life, forever. Nothing, not even the direst penury, would induce her to have anything to do with him again.

On rejoining the company at luncheon, she was relieved to see that Mr. Ravensworth was absent. The Duchess, who might otherwise have questioned, was happily celebrating the recovery of her dog, which she had feared to have been at death's door. She made a civil enquiry, to which Theodora returned a noncommittal answer and a sincere word of thanks for the use of the chaise, then returned to her recital of the pet's antics.

Evening brought Mr. Ravensworth again. Theodora stayed as close as she could to Lady Anne Fitzroy, which tactic he observed with only the smallest lift of his mobile eyebrow. Theodora, alert to his every expression, did not miss this, and promptly changed her seat, moving to an isolated chair. To her annoyance he made no attempt to follow and speak to her, and, feeling rather foolish, she returned to the gathering again.

It was some while later that she turned from a conversation with "Monk" Lewis, and found Ravensworth at her elbow.

"I hope you didn't speak as roughly to him as you do to me? He is very sensitive, you know. One does not even need to speak harshly to him to provoke his tears. He was once found crying, after dinner here, and said it was because the Duchess spoke so very kindly to him."

"Mr. Lewis? Of course I did not. At least, I don't think so. I do not know why you must always insist on recalling the times I have lost my temper with you, Mr. Ravensworth. It is not something I am proud of, but I have to say that on each occasion you have been at least as much to blame as I, if not more."

"I admit it! I should not tease you, I know, but I like to see your beautiful eyes sparkle in that charming way." Theodora was not used to compliments from him, and searched his face to see whether this was another form of teasing. "Do not look so puzzled! Have I really treated you so badly that you cannot believe me sincere when I tell you you are so beautiful?"

To her annoyance she found herself blushing, but her pride made her refuse to drop her eyes. "It is a novel experience," she said with an attempt at lightness.

"To be told that you are beautiful? Surely not."

"No, but..." She laughed. "Now you have me sounding like the most self-satisfied of creatures! What I mean is that I am not used to receiving pretty speeches from you, Mr. Ravensworth."

"And you are not sure that you like it?"

"Not very sure."

"Then I shall turn the subject, in my most gentleman-like fashion. How did your visit to your great-uncle turn out?"

"That is a subject I like even less."

"There is no pleasing you," he said plaintively. "I cannot, of course, force you to confide in me, but, as you have pointed out that I am at least in part responsible for his invitation, I cannot but feel an element of curiosity. Was it very bad?"

"Horrid. The house is dark, and dirty, and he is—oh, I don't know—dark and dirty too, I suppose. Not in his looks—though he was not very clean—but in himself, if you know what I mean."

"I do. I am sorry that you have had such an ordeal."

"So am I, but I do not mean to think of it any more. He is nothing to me, and I never will see him again."

"Did he want you to?"

The need to confide in someone was very great, and on this subject she might not even speak to her mother.

"Yes. He offered me his fortune."

"And you said?" prompted Ravensworth.

"Well, naturally I went down on my knees and accepted it! What do you think?" she flashed.

"I think that you probably spurned his fortune much as you once spurned my kisses. Did you break his leg? He must be pretty old, and I, of course, was protected by my riding boots."

His teasing had the effect that he had intended—of distracting her from the sting of the memory. She gave a small smile and he saw the tensed muscles in her shoulder and back relax.

"Only you have the ability—and the desire—to provoke me into actual violence, Mr. Ravensworth. I think I was able to leave him in no doubt of my feelings, without resorting to physical means."

"Indeed? He is a fortunate man, then."

"Because I did not injure him? You do not really think I would do such a thing?"

"No. Fortunate, that he is in no doubt of your feelings."

Thinking that she had misheard, or misunderstood, she looked up at him in surprise, but he was already turning away. She made no attempt to prevent his leaving her, but remained as she was for some moments, looking very thoughtful. A slow tide of blood ebbed over her cheeks, and she brought her fan into play.

The following day saw her return to London. The Duchess bade her farewell with great cordiality, and invited her to return in May to the celebration for her birthday.

"You must come, my dear. All my friends will be here, and I hope to have the King, too, if he is well enough."

"Does he attend parties, madam?"

"Sometimes, if it is to people he knows and likes. Of course he talks a great deal, but one must not mind him, for he is very gentle, and means so well, the dear man! Do say you will come!"

"I should be honoured, of course."

"Your rich uncle will like that, I shouldn't wonder!"

"He will not know of it, surely, madam. We do not correspond."

"Not know of it? How do you think he knew you were here in the first place? The servants, my dear. They always know everything—don't ask me how. He is bound to find out, and why not? Do you have some objection to inheriting a fortune?"

"From him, madam, yes, I do," said Theodora, greatly daring. "I would rather go in rags."

"Foolish child. You do not know what you are saying," was the careless reply. Theodora merely curtsied. One did not argue with a Princess.

Lady Lingdale was agog to hear about the visit. Theodora went through the whole time, almost minute by minute, describing the rooms, the clothes, the food, and the people.

She omitted only to mention the subject of Mr. Bellerby. She might have guessed, however, that she could not keep such a secret. Word of their interesting encounter, though not, of course, of its outcome, had spread among her acquaintance, carried by other guests from Oatlands. Lady Lingdale was triumphant. Here was the reward for her generosity to her young guest! She did not mention it to her, but in the privacy of her own room she spent some happy moments calculating the extent of Jonas Bellerby's wealth, and his age, and how long he was likely to survive.

Edmund dined with them that evening. Lady Lingdale had decided to dine at home, *en famille,* so that she could hear and enjoy all the details of Oatlands, and she had decreed her son's presence. Of late he had been going out alone a good deal, returning very late at night, and sleeping late in the morning, so that she had hardly seen him. While Theodora had been away his mother had not attempted to prevent him, but, now that her charge was home, gilded with reflected glory of Royalty and with the prospect of an inheritance, she was determined that he should not waste his opportunities.

There was so much to talk about that Theodora was not, at first, aware that he was very silent. Towards the end of the meal a chance remark of his mother's drew her attention to the fact that he had hardly eaten anything, only picking at the food on his plate, and waving away most of the dishes offered to him.

Theodora might have thought no more of this than that he was affecting a romantic air, and studying to keep his slender figure, if she had not then remarked the extreme pallor of his face, the shadows under his eyes, and the little pucker of strain and worry that tightened the skin of that white brow. She said nothing, but later in the evening had an opportunity to speak to him.

Edmund had not rejoined them very quickly after they had withdrawn from the dining-room, but had sat in solitary state, and it did not take any great perspicacity to see that he had been imbibing freely of the port while he remained at the table. His speech and his walk were both normal, but with the studied carefulness of one who feared that his words or his feet might at any moment become inextricably entangled. Lady Lingdale, with a lack of subtlety which would at any other time have made Theodora giggle, had made an excuse to go and leave them alone together, which provided her with a perfect opportunity.

"Is anything the matter, Edmund?" she asked, breaking in on a long-winded account of a play he had seen earlier in the week, which she suspected was intended to distract her.

"The matter? What should be the matter?" He did not meet her eyes.

"I thought you might be worried about something. You did not eat any dinner, and it seems to me that you are not as well as you used to be. Does your leg still pain you?"

"What leg? Oh, I see. No, I never feel it. I expect I am a little tired, that is all. Not used to this London life, you know."

His expression was hunted, and she forbore to press him. She was not deceived, though, and when Lady Lingdale returned, putting her head coyly round the door as if fearing—or hoping—to interrupt some tender scene, she soon made an excuse of feeling sleepy after the excitement of the last few days, and went up to her room. Somehow the forced cheerfulness of Edmund's talk made her worry about him more than ever, and she determined to find out what was wrong. She had become aware that his feelings for her had modified, and had been much relieved, but as a friend she felt anxious for his happiness.

Could it be that he had fallen in love with some other girl, and feared telling her, and his mother, about it? True, she had never seen him pay particular attention to any other young lady. His manner to herself, which had begun by being almost comically possessive, had ebbed to the friendly care of a brother, much to her pleasure. Lady Lingdale, she knew, still harboured hopes, which would undoubtedly intensify when she learned of Theodora's invitation to visit the rich, miserly Mr. Bellerby.

The following morning she made sure of being up and at the breakfast table in good time. Lady Lingdale seldom or never put in an appearance until much later, preferring to take her cup of chocolate in the privacy of her room, and not emerging until her first toilette had been made. At first, Theodora feared that she would not be joined by Edmund either, but at last the door opened. He looked taken aback when he saw her, and would almost have gone away, but she greeted him with calm good humour, and made trivial conversation about the weather, and their future invitations, while he joined her at the table.

Examining him covertly, she did not think that he had enjoyed a good night's repose. The shadows under his eyes were as dark as ever, and his heavy eyelids betokened a sleepless night. He ate little, but drank the cup of coffee she gave him, and a second which, unasked, she poured. His replies to her friendly chatter were disjointed, and he did not appear to notice when she fell silent, but sat, elbow on table, resting his head on his hand.

"You should not take so much port, if it gives you a headache, Edmund," she suggested gently.

"What? Oh, yes, the port. I did take rather a lot. Yes, it has given me a bit of a head today."

She accepted the excuse, and said nothing while one of the servants came in with a pile of letters. Among them were several obvious invitations, addressed to Lady Lingdale but which she did not scruple to open, on that lady's previous instructions, to see who had sent them. Distracted by this pleasant occupation, she did not see that Edmund had cast aside most of his letters, and opened only one. Now he stood up so abruptly that his chair crashed to the floor behind him. Theodora jumped and exclaimed, but one look at his face had her out of her chair almost as quickly, and hurrying to his side.

"Edmund! What is it? Are you ill? My dear, do not look like that!" His face was livid white, and at his feet the piece of paper, scarcely whiter, fluttered innocuously where he had let it fall. He turned sightless eyes on her, but did not speak. The servant, attracted by the noise, hurried in, but Theodora quickly righted the chair.

"It is all right, James! Only his lordship's chair! It gave me such a start, but no harm is done." She continued to talk in a soft, even tone until the servant had gone, then she took Edmund by the arms and gave him a little shake.

"Come, now, Edmund. It is no use thinking you can fob me off with excuses, and tell me everything is all right! Sit down before you fall down, and tell me what has happened."

He sat down at once, with an obedience that she found very touching. Pulling her own chair closer, she sat also, keeping his hand firmly gripped between her own. A little colour was returning to his face and his eyes were more aware.

"Oh, Dora. I am ruined," he said simply, and to her horror his eyes filled with tears.

"Ruined? Nonsense," she replied firmly. Sympathy, at this point, would do more harm than good, and only provoke a display of sensibility that would achieve nothing, and would be difficult to hide from the servants.

"Yes, I am. Ruined." His eyes strayed to the letter, still lying on the carpet. She leaned down to pick it up and, when he did not demur, read it swiftly. It was a politely worded note, reminding Lord Lingdale that his debts should be paid at once, and reminding him also that anything incurred during a card game was a debt of honour. The name at the bottom was unknown to her.

"You have a gaming debt," she said, a statement, not a question. He nodded. "Is it a great deal?"

He nodded miserably, but could not bring himself to speak.

"How much, then?"

He took a shaky breath. "Five thousand pounds." The words came out so low that she could not be sure she had heard him aright.

"Five...?"

"Five thousand pounds," he repeated in louder tones. Theodora looked at him in horror.

"Edmund! How did you...? I mean, surely you cannot have intended...?"

"I don't know." His tone was despairing. His face dropped into his hands, and his voice was muffled. "I don't really remember. I suppose I was a bit drunk, but not so much! Just merry, you know. I was playing, and the cards seemed to be running in my favour. Everyone was egging me on, and when I started to lose I didn't take it very seriously. I thought, you see, that it was just a run of bad luck, and it would be bound to turn soon. Then it carried on, and I knew I had lost more than I could afford."

"So you stopped then?" She knew the answer already.

"No!" he groaned. "I must have been mad! But I thought—oh, I don't know what. That somehow I would win enough to pay off what I had lost, for I knew I could not raise the money. But things just got worse and worse. By the end, I had lost count of what I had wagered. When it was added up, I nearly died. But what was I to do? A debt of honour, you see."

"But surely, if you told him you were unable to pay...?"

"Impossible!"

Theodora thought that she had never heard of anything so silly, but she knew that this was yet another manly foible that she could not expect to understand.

"Well, then. If it must be paid, it must. Have you any money at all? I have about fifty pounds still left. It's not much, I know, but it's a beginning."

He looked at her in horror.

"Take your money? I would not dream of it."

"For goodness' sake try not to be so foolish," she begged him. "What is the alternative?"

"I would have to flee the country, I suppose."

"And only think how happy that would make me, and your mama," she pointed out acidly. "I suppose Lady Lingdale—?"

"She would give me what she could, I know, but she has next to nothing. She is never very beforehand with the world, you know, and recently she has been spending more than usual on her gowns."

"Then it must be Mr. Ravensworth."

Edmund jumped to his feet again. "Never!" he exclaimed.

"But he is so wealthy—a sum like that cannot possibly signify to him! Besides, he is your guardian, and I expect you lost the money at one of those horrid gaming clubs he has introduced you to."

"Yes, I did, but that's beside the point. Everyone goes to them."

"Not everyone loses five thousand pounds at one sitting," she pointed out.

"Well, they do, then!" he retorted, stung. "At least, not everyone, but I know for a fact that Alvanley dropped nearly fifteen thousand, only last month!"

"You are proposing to model yourself on Lord Alvanley, then? He may be able to afford to live in such style, but you, I am sure, cannot."

"Nor can he. They say he's nearly been rolled up several times already."

"Oh, why are we discussing Lord Alvanley's debts, when it is yours we must consider? I still say you should go to Mr. Ravensworth. It has seemed to me, recently, that he is perhaps not quite so harsh as you once thought him," she said.

"I expect that's all a front," he replied.

"Come, now, Edmund, you do not really believe all that stuff you were telling me before, about how your cousin wishes you ill? I tell you frankly that it is the moonshine."

He had the grace to look abashed.

"Oh, for that, I know it is. But that doesn't mean he's any friend of mine."

"You cannot believe that he would want it said that his ward was forced to flee the country a bankrupt because he would not lift a finger to help, when he is one of the richest men in England? Whatever he might have done to you in the past, I do not think you would punish him like that. He would never be able to hold up his head again."

"You've very quick to defend him, Theodora."

"Not at all. Simply, I cannot understand your scruples in this matter. Surely it is an easy enough thing? I do not say that he should give you the money, only that he should lend it, and when you come of age you may repay him."

"I know, I know. Do you imagine I have not been thinking about this, day and night? But I cannot do it,

Theodora. I cannot ask him to lend me the money. I know you cannot understand it, but you do not know him as I do. You do not know how he can be. That damned sarcastic tongue of his, it's enough to flay the skin from your body!'' He shuddered. ''I know it of old. Call me craven if you will, but I cannot do it.''

She knew that it was true. His sensitive spirit, so different from Ravensworth's forceful intelligence, was not proof against his guardian's words. Accepting defeat on this front, she was not prepared to give up altogether.

''Well, then, all right. Is there no other way you can get the money? Can one not borrow?''

His tone was weary.

''Don't you think I haven't tried that already. They will not lend money without security, particularly to someone of my age. And I have no security.''

''Surely your country house? Oh, I suppose it is all entailed?''

''Precisely. It is very good of you, Theodora, but I am afraid you cannot help me.''

''I'm not so sure.'' She spoke slowly, choosing her words with care. ''This security, what does it entail?''

''I don't know.''

''What I mean is, it doesn't have to be an actual object, does it? If you were able to tell them, for instance, that you will inherit a fortune one day, would that be enough?''

''Yes, if I could prove it. Unfortunately, I cannot.''

''What if you could tell them you were engaged to an heiress?''

''That would do the trick too. Again, the same unfortunate difficulty applies. Even to save myself, I do not think I can accomplish such a thing quite as quickly as that. Besides, word soon gets around, you know. I don't see any heiress accepting me, knowing that I'm up to my ears in debt.''

"That's just where you're wrong! You may tell them you are engaged to *me!*"

His look of horror was so comical that at any other time Theodora would have fallen into laughter.

"But I thought you said—"

"Yes, I did! I don't mean we need actually marry, ninny! Merely that we should announce our engagement so that you may borrow the money. Then, when we have worked out some way of repaying it, which I am sure we will be able to do, we may say it was all a mistake!"

She smiled sunnily. The unnerving suspicion that she had run mad crossed his mind, and he looked at her closely.

"Pray do not stare at me like that! I think, since I have been so immodest as practically to propose to you, you should at least express your gratitude!"

"Oh, yes! That is, of course I am very grateful, and—and honoured, and all that. And I know I said I wanted to—and naturally, nothing could be more—but..." He floundered to a halt. Theodora giggled, and he eyed her with distinct disfavour.

"I wish you will pay attention, Edmund! I am not trying to get you to marry me—have I not always said we should not suit? This is no more than a ruse, to help you out of your fix."

"Yes, yes, I believe you! But Theodora, consider! You are a lovely girl, but you are not an heiress! And do not think that we can deceive them on this matter, for I can assure you they are very well informed."

"Better informed than you, I hope. You have not heard, then, that I am my great-uncle's only living relative—apart from Mama, of course, and they fell out years ago."

"Your great-uncle?"

"Well, step-great-uncle, then. Jonas Bellerby."

"Jonas Bellerby? Good heavens, I have heard of him."

"Congratulations. Then you know that he is even richer than Mr. Ravensworth?"

"Yes, but Theodora, he may be your relative, but that does not mean to say he will leave you anything, does it?"

"Probably not. What you do not know, though, is that I visited him, just the other day. He lives near Oatlands, and he sent to invite me. Horrid old snob! The Duchess saw his letter, and insisted that I should go. I own, I did not at all want to, but how glad I am that I did! For you may depend upon it that word will soon spread!"

"And he is going to leave you his fortune?" Edmund was almost gasping for breath.

"Oh, no, I told him I didn't want it!" she replied blithely, unaware that she had deprived him of speech. "But he thinks I did not really mean it, for he cannot believe anyone can resist the lure of his horrid bags of gold. Anyway, it does not signify, for you may be sure that the mere fact of my visit will be enough! He is practically a recluse, and sees nobody, you know!"

Edmund sat gaping at her for so long, quite silent, that at length Theodora quite lost her patience with him.

"Well? Shall we be engaged or not?"

Edmund jumped to his feet.

"You are quite sure? I mean, there is no one else? I own I have sometimes wondered whether you and my—" Her eyes flashed at him, and he tactfully turned his last word into a cough. "Sorry. Quite forgotten what I was saying. Well, Dora, I do not see how I can refuse. If you are quite sure, and, of course, I would not dream of holding you to anything, if ever . . . Yes. Well. Oh, thank you, Dora!"

His gratitude impelled him to take her boldly into his arms. Dizzy with relief, he kissed her cheek, repeating the embrace several times because he was so happy he hardly knew what he was doing. She stood quite unembarrassed in his hold, inclining her cheek with friendly composure.

It was at this inauspicious moment that the door opened, and Ravensworth walked in.

Theodora stiffened, and would have pulled out of his arms, but Edmund was still delirious with joy.

"Cousin Ravensworth! You may congratulate me! Dora has made me the happiest of men!"

It was quite true, and the happiness was clearly to be seen in his face, though the cause was not quite what his guardian thought.

"Congratulate you? I certainly do, Edmund. What very quick work, to be sure. Miss Waverton, I wish you every happiness."

He advanced to shake his ward's outstreched hand. Turning to Theodora, he merely bowed.

"Well, I wanted to know what your feelings were, and now I do, don't I? I shall not be foolish enough to express such a wish again." His eyes were cold, hardly seeming to look at her. Theodora opened frozen lips to speak, but he was gone.

CHAPTER ELEVEN

EDMUND WAS SO ELATED that he noticed nothing. If Theodora had not restrained him, he would have rushed off there and then to the moneylenders, but she gently pointed out the advisability of informing his mama first of all, and asking her to draft a notice to the papers. He concurred at once, and Theodora was then called upon to endure the raptures of Lady Lingdale, whose delight knew no bounds, particularly when her son let slip, in an artistically casual fashion, that Theodora had actually visited her wealthy relative so recently. Edmund found it hard to keep his patience, but was at length dismissed when he said that he needed to go out.

"You will be wishing to buy a gift for dearest Theodora!" she beamed. "Not a ring, of course, for there is the one your dear papa gave me, which I have always intended for you to use! But some other keepsake, to mark the happy event! If you are in need of funds, dear boy..." she hinted delicately, and, with a stricken look at his betrothed, Edmund accepted a generous banknote, firmly resolving that the gift should be repaid as soon as possible. With a few exhortations and several more kisses, he was allowed to leave, and the full force of her ladyship's joy was turned on Theodora.

"My dear, dear child!" Lady Lingdale said, patting the cushions on the sofa next to her. "Come and sit by me, and let us be cosy together. How happy I am! How very, very happy! I little thought, when my dear Lingdale was taken from me, that I should ever feel so happy again!''

A few real tears sparkled on her cheeks, and Theodora felt her own eyes filling. Never before had she felt so uncomfortable, so guilty. Only the fact that she knew she would never knowingly inherit Jonas Bellerby's wealth made it possible for her to restrain herself from throwing herself at her hostess's feet and confessing all. As it was she wiped her eyes, gritted her teeth, and resolutely set herself to please Lady Lingdale, while uttering as few untruths as was humanly possible.

Fortunately for her already tender conscience, Lady Lingdale's maternal partiality led her to extol her son, which praise Theodora was only too happy to join in, merely attempting to stem the flood of reminiscence and exaggeration when they threatened to overwhelm the lady once more with happy tears. At last, with the excuse that she must write to her own mother at once, she was able to leave the lady to her happy musings, and to the pleasant task of writing out the necessary announcement to the papers.

Alone in her room, Theodora sat with a blank sheet of paper in front of her, and chewed the end of her pen in lieu of her fingernails as was now her custom. Impossible not to tell her the truth, that loving and loved mother who waited, no doubt with great anxiety, to hear news of her daughter. But how to explain her actions; how, above all, to write anything at all when a cold, angry face was so persistently interposing itself between her eyes and the desk? The paper blurred before her eyes, and she put down her much abused pen, and, pushing back her chair, left the table and fled to her bed.

Curling up childishly on the covers, she ran through her mind what he had said. There was no need to put a name to that "he": ever since she had known those fierce kisses, so different from Edmund's chaste and brotherly salute, there had been no man in her heart, she now acknowledged, but Alexander Ravensworth.

Had he not said, on their drive to Richmond, that he would never permit her to marry Edmund? At first she had taken this for the merest snobbery, irritating but petty, and then for dislike, because they never seemed to meet without falling into some disagreement. Now she thought back, and realised that his actual words had been that he would do his utmost to prevent her marrying his ward. He had also said, she recalled, that his reasons might lay him open to ridicule. He had been kind, she thought now, and had not taken offence when she was rude to him. Come to think of it, he never had done. Until now.

Her cold hands pressed to hot cheeks, Theodora scarcely believed the evidence of her own memory. His choice of words now seemed to her peculiarly significant, allied to his later remark about wishing he knew about her own feelings. He could not, surely, mean that he himself was attracted to her? For all her innocence, she knew very well that a man might kiss many women without loving them, though she now acknowledged, almost shamefaced even when admitting it to herself, that with her it was far otherwise. Nothing in her life, not even that unpleasant visit to her great-uncle, had ever hurt her so much as the sight of that withdrawn face, those bleak eyes that had rested on her so stonily. The knowledge that nothing could be simpler than to tell him the truth was no use to her; however misguided she might think him, Edmund's wishes on this subject must be paramount.

What might happen in the future, she could scarcely bear to think. That Edmund, once his debt of honour was paid, would do his utmost to repay the moneylender, was certain. What was equally certain, however, was that he would be completely unable to do so for a very long time.

For how long would she be expected to keep up this masquerade? It would be two years before Edmund gained control of his fortune; surely she would not have to carry on for that long, and, if she did, would anyone believe in so long an engagement, that never seemed to lead to a marriage? Lady Lingdale would have something to say on that subject, she was sure.

It occurred to her that she had acted in haste, and true to the adage must repent at leisure. It had seemed such a good idea at the time, she wondered why these objections had not occurred to her sooner. At the same time, she felt bound to help poor Edmund, and she supposed that if she had it all to do again she would probably behave in the same way. Drying her eyes, she returned resolutely to her pen, and struggled to write a cheerful, confiding, but not too revealing letter to Lady Waverton.

By the time she had finished this delicate task Edmund had returned, and she was able to get him to frank her letter. He gave her a very pretty brooch, of pearls and sapphires, which she was embarrassed to accept.

"But Edmund . . . I should not!" she demurred.

"Nonsense, my dear child," put in Lady Lingdale, fondly looking on. "Of course he must make you a gift. Very prettily chosen, Edmund! A most suitable offering!"

Blushing with embarrassment, Edmund bent to pin the gift to her gown, taking the opportunity to whisper in her ear, "All's done! It's paid!"

Theodora could only look her pleasure, and privately resolve that the valuable gift should be returned as soon as possible. Lady Lingdale had given her son her engagement ring, set with very fine diamonds, and this he placed on her finger. To her relief it was much too large, which gave her an excuse not to wear it at least for a day or two. Under his mother's expectant gaze, he bent to salute her

cheek, which passionless embrace Theodora accepted,
quelling a desire to giggle.

During the following days Theodora had to endure, with
becoming modesty, the good wishes and—usually—con-
cealed envy of her female acquaintance, and the chagrin,
real or imaginary, of those who had been accustomed to
think of themselves as her court. Lady Lingdale, over-
flowing with good humour, was set on giving a large party
to celebrate the engagement. Theodora, horrified that her
hostess should spend so much money on such a thing, was
only able to halt her feverish plans by pointing out that her
own mother would be unlikely to be able to attend such a
gathering.

"Of course, I should have thought," said Lady Lingdale at once, all contrition. "My dearest child, I would not
for worlds so slight your dear mama! But you think she
would not come?"

"I am very sure of it, ma'am," replied Theodora with a
firmness she did not feel. "But it would make me so sad,
to think of attending such a gathering without having her
at my side! Perhaps, in a few months, when she has had
time to grow accustomed to the idea of appearing in public..."

"Naturally! It is only too understandable, and like your
sweet nature, dear one, to think of it! But something must
be done to mark the occasion. Do you think just a small
family gathering, to introduce you to Edmund's relations? They are a dull lot, by and large, I am afraid, but
nevertheless it would be expected that they should be invited to meet you."

"Of course," returned Theodora with a sinking heart.
Of a crowd of ancient aunts and distant cousins she had no
fear; one cousin, however, she felt a reluctance almost
amounting to dread at the thought of encountering.

Of Ravensworth there was neither sight nor sound, though it did not occur to Edmund, dizzy with relief at his escape, to wonder at it. Theodora, who could think of little else, fretted in silence. She could not bring herself to ask whether he had accepted Lady Lingdale's invitation, but knew that, had he refused it, there must have been much remark made.

On the evening of the party she had to pinch her cheeks and bite her lips to bring a little colour into them, and she was glad that her long white kid gloves hid the clammy coldness of her hands. Uncles, aunts, and cousins passed by in a moving daze of faces and smiles. She supposed she was responding normally, and that the words that she forced herself to utter made some kind of sense, for no one looked at her askance.

The minutes crept by, and still Ravensworth did not arrive. Theodora began to allow herself to hope—he had unexpectedly been called away to some distant place, like Australia; or perhaps he was so little interested in his ward's affairs that he had forgotten to come.

Her hopes were in vain. Glancing up from a conversation, carried on in stentorian tones by a very deaf and ancient female cousin, she saw the familiar tall figure approaching. He looked larger than usual, she thought, and his face still wore the cold, distant look that she had seen on it before. She drew a deep breath to still the trembling of her limbs, and a moment later he was bowing over her hand.

"Mr. Ravensworth! What a delightful surprise!" she said inanely. If he felt the trembling of her hand in his, he made no sign, but released it as quickly as he could.

"Naturally I would wish to be present at so happy an event," he replied smoothly.

"You are very kind." She fell silent.

"Have you set a date for the wedding?" His eyes were focused slightly to one side and beyond her face.

"Oh, no, not yet!" she responded nervously. "Not for some while yet. There is Mama, you see, and..." Her voice tailed off.

"Quite. Well, Miss Waverton, I must hope that you will have more influence than I have done, in encouraging Edmund to lead a sensible life."

Her eyes flew to his face in a panic-stricken look, and she gave a little start. Could it be that he knew already of Edmund's debt? If so, she need not have entered into this charade.

"What—what do you mean?"

Arrested by her tremulous manner, for the first time his eyes looked properly at her. A small frown creased his forehead and drew his dark eyebrows together.

"Why, merely that he will give up these ridiculous pretensions of being a poet, and settle down to normal family life!"

"Oh. Oh, yes, of course." He looked at her more closely, aware for the first time of something other than his own feelings of chagrin and jealousy.

"Is anything the matter, Theodora?" His gentler tone made her feel even worse, but she swallowed the sudden tightness that constricted her throat, and forced her lips into a bright smile.

"The matter? Oh, no, Mr. Ravensworth! What could give you such an idea? I am so happy, you can't imagine!"

"No. I can't," he returned shortly, in his former chilly tones. "I am sure you deserve everything that you are feeling, Miss Waverton. And now I see my old uncle Tobias beckoning me, and must leave you for the present."

He was gone, and at once her smile vanished. As she thought over his parting words she had to fight back the tears that would have flooded her eyes and rolled down her cheeks. That she deserved everything she felt was no more than the truth, but it did not make it any easier to bear. For the rest of the evening he kept his distance from her, and made his farewells in the most formal and hurried fashion.

April passed into May. It brought a letter from Lady Waverton, filled with unexpressed anxiety and heavy with unspoken words. It also brought, as time passed, the Duchess of York's birthday, which great event had completely slipped Theodora's mind, so that the invitation, which included Edmund as her betrothed, came as a surprise. Less welcome than either of these, it also brought a letter from Jonas Bellerby.

No less terse than before, it stated that news had reached him of her engagement to Lord Lingdale.

You do not ask my consent, so I take this opportunity to tell you that I am absolutely against this match. The young man has little or no fortune, and even less standing in the world. Worse than all this, it has come to my attention that he has been using my name, *my name*, to raise money, doubtless to pay off his debts. If your mother's history has not taught you to beware of gamblers, then I must perform the office. If you wed this young profligate, not a penny piece will you get from me, and so I will inform the world, if necessary.

As before, the letter in its crabbed hand was signed, without benefit of closing compliments, with his name, Jonas Bellerby.

Theodora read it with rising anger and, by the end of it, dismay. After all their stratagems, that it should come to this! Edmund would be not only ruined, but made to look a fool or, worse, a fortune-hunter. She could not even tell him of it, for there was nothing he could do. In the turmoil of her mind, all she could think of was that somehow she must visit the old man herself, and contrive to arrange things.

How to get there was the problem—impossible to ask for the use of the carriage, to go such a long journey, without some kind of reasonable explanation. The only answer was to do as she had done before, and visit him from Oatlands. She must make the Duchess's party her opportunity, and hope that in so great a crowd her absence would not be remarked.

It was certainly one of the first great events of the Season, and Theodora, driving with an excited Edmund to Oatlands, could only wish that she were in a better mood to enjoy it. The weather was fine and seasonable, which was all to the good, and in her simple white tiffany gown she hoped to attract little notice. As they alighted she managed to make an opportunity to return, on the pretext of something forgotten, and speak rapidly to the coachman, warning him to be at the ready, as it was possible that she might have need of him before long.

The gardens, opulently beautiful, were already thronged. Not only the great and the noble, but local tenants and labourers were bidden to the celebration, and Theodora saw the great tables, each burdened with six quarts of punch, laid out for them to join in the feasting, and drink to the Duchess's health on this, her forty-fifth birthday.

Edmund, who had never seen anything quite like it, was much struck, and Theodora forgot some of her nagging worry in showing him the gardens and the grotto. To his fascination and delight, the King and all the Princesses had come down from Windsor. The King, now seventy-three, delighted all his well-wishers by walking about quite hap-

pily and normally, and little pools of conjecture and speculation followed him as he pursued his way, his well-known
ejaculation of "What! What!" ringing out. After all, he
had before made a recovery—maybe he would do so again,
and what a disappointment then for the Regent!

"There is Mr. Brummell," pointed out Theodora. "Do
you see him? How very elegant he looks."

Edmund cast a doubtful eye down his own slender
frame. The buttons of his coat, of which he had been so
proud, looked suddenly vulgarly large and ostentatious
when he looked at the Beau's.

"You look very elegant, too," added Theodora, notic-
ing his glance. He was pleased, but wished that she would
not address him in the tone an indulgent nurse might use
to a child in her charge. Brummell walked by, surrounded
by cronies and hangers-on. He spared a smile and a small
bow for Theodora, but did not halt. They heard his voice
floating back to them with its own peculiar clarity of tone.

"If the Prince does not behave himself, I shall bring the
old King again into fashion."

"Did you hear that?" whispered Edmund. "He has a
nerve, I will say that of him."

"It is no more than the truth," said Theodora indignantly. "He could do it, if he wanted to, you know. I think
that is at the root of why the Regent is annoyed with him.
He has been wanting to give a large party, like this one, to
celebrate his new status, but with the King so much improved he has had to postpone it."

"I must say, Theodora, sometimes I think you are
treating me like some straw-chewing yokel from the country," complained Edmund. "I know you have stayed here,
and are bosom friends with the Beau, but there is no need
to explain things to me. I hear all the gossip at my club."

"I beg your pardon, Edmund. I did not mean to sound so patronising. I am afraid my mind is all at sixes and sevens, today, and I scarcely know what I am saying."

"Well, it's all right," he said ungraciously, "only don't do it again. I say! There's old Tom over there! I haven't seen him for ages!"

Welcoming the distraction, Theodora disengaged her hand from his arm.

"Why don't you go and join him? I am poor company at the moment, and I think I have a little headache coming on. I will go and sit down in the shade, for a while, and see you later."

He was eager to be gone, but aware of his duties. "You are unwell? Would you like me to take you home?"

Nothing could have been further from her wishes. "Oh, no, Edmund! I am quite well. It is all the bustle, and the heat, and the excitement. I shall be very well presently, if I may find some quiet corner out of the sun. It is so warm for May!"

He looked at her anxiously, noting for the first time her pallor, and the shadows beneath her eyes.

"You don't look too good, and that's a fact!"

"Well, thank you, Edmund. You certainly know how to fill a young lady with confidence."

"I didn't mean—"

"I know you didn't. I was teasing you."

"May I not fetch you a drink, or at least sit with you? I do not like to leave you like this."

"Oh, for heaven's sake, Edmund, stop fussing!" she said with a spurt of anger. "I shall be perfectly all right, if you will only go away and leave me alone!"

He saw that she was in earnest, and left her near a grove of trees, where she said she would find a cool, quiet place to rest. Watching him leave, she saw him reach his friends, and knew that within a few minutes she would be forgotten. Without another backward glance, she slipped away from the throng.

It was cool and quiet beneath the trees, and with some relief she made for a rustic seat, empty at present, and sat down on it. It would not do for her to disappear too soon, for fear that Edmund might take it into his head to come and look for her. From her vantage point, she could see the approach of unwelcome people, and take evasive action; also, she could make her way to the stables without going back into the crowd. The newly opened leaves, rustling above her, brought peaceful childhood memories to her, as did the clean balsam scent of the air. Half dreaming, half awake, she sat at peace.

Since her arrival, she had half hoped, half feared, to see Ravensworth. He was almost certain to be there, for though she had heard no word of him since her engagement she was sure he had not left London, since he must surely have notified Lady Lingdale, at least, if such had been his intention. Once or twice she thought she had glimpsed his tall form, in the distance, but she could not be sure of it. She was not to know that he was only too aware of her presence, and watched her every move with a jealous attention which might, if she had known of it, have made her very much happier.

His own shock, on learning of her betrothal, had been severe. While he was not a coxcomb, he was well aware of the attraction he had for women, and he was moderately sure that he would be able, when he was ready, to call her to his side. That she might have serious designs on his ward had never, since the beginning, crossed his mind. He was well aware that, sheltered though her upbringing might have been, she was still more mature, mentally, by several years than Edmund.

When he had seen her in Edmund's arms, the fire had risen in him so that it was with difficulty that he had restrained himself from attacking the young man, and half his anger with Theodora was that she was able, without conscious effort, to make him come so near to losing his self-control.

Since that moment he had done his best to put her out of his mind. His anger was all the greater because he had found himself quite unable to do so, no matter how he attempted to distract himself. Now he was aware of her, from the first moment of her arrival, and, despite himself though he did, he found himself studying her face with jealous greed. What he saw gave him pause for thought. Unlike Edmund, he saw at once her pallor, her look of someone who had not slept and who had something to worry about. When she sent Edmund off, after so short a time, and withdrew under the trees, he made his way at once to his ward's side.

That young man, he noticed sourly, was in no way perturbed to be without his affianced bride, but was talking and laughing without a care in the world.

"Good day, Edmund." He infused as much cordiality as he could into his greeting, and Lord Lingdale, who was inclined to take most things at their face value, turned to him cheerfully.

"Why, good day, Cousin Ravensworth! I have not seen you for ages! What a splendid party this is, is it not? Have you seen the King? And did you know there are to be fireworks, later?"

Suppressing his impatience, Ravensworth acknowledged that he was aware of both these entertainments.

"I have never been to anything like it before!" Edmund enthused on. "It is so very kind of the Duchess to invite me. I have never seen anything so fine as these gardens. Of course, you must know them well, but they really are beautiful."

"I am sure the Duchess would be pleased to know that you are so impressed," remarked Ravensworth. "Have you met her yet?" he added, with studied carelessness.

"No, for she does not know me. I expect Theodora will introduce me, if there is a chance," replied his ward with maddening imperturbability. Ravensworth glanced round the group, affecting to notice for the first time that Theodora was absent.

"Ah, Theodora! She is not with you?"

"No, she was finding the heat and the crowds trying. I left her over there, by the trees."

"You did not feel the need to stay with her?"

"Oh, no! She was quite cross, you know, and sent me away. She did not want me to stay with her."

"You did not mind, I suppose? This is not some lovers' tiff?"

Edmund stared at him with surprise.

"Lovers' tiff? That's a good one! I must tell her about that!" He roared with laughter, and Ravensworth again stifled the urge to take him by his carefully arranged neckcloth and shake him.

"I mean, she really does not mind you leaving her, and enjoying yourself without her?"

"Oh, no, Dora never cares about that sort of thing. She is the best of good fellows!" This loverly encomium deprived his guardian of speech for a moment. "She finds me annoying, you know," he confided cheerfully.

"She is not alone in that. Does this not bode ill for your future life together?"

"Life together? But that's not...oh, of course, I forgot. When we are married, you mean?"

"Just so," said Ravensworth, who was beginning to look very thoughtful. "*When* you are married."

"Oh, as to that, I have no worries," replied Edmund with some care. Experience had taught him to beware when his guardian's eyes took on that particular intent look. An uncanny ability to read a person's mind, when that person had something he would have preferred to keep quiet about, was one of the things Edmund as a boy had most disliked about his cousin.

"I see." Ravensworth said no more, but the two men regarded one another for a few moments. Then the older man smiled.

"Well, I will not keep you from your enjoyment of the party. Remind me to introduce you to Princess Fred, if Theodora does not do so."

Unnerved by this unexpected friendliness, Lord Lingdale watched Ravensworth striding away, without apparent haste, but making a path through the crowd as easily as the prow of a boat sliced through small waves. He was soon lost to sight, and Edmund, frowning for a moment in thought, allowed himself to be distracted by his friends.

Ravensworth, making a circuitous way back to the grove of trees where he had last seen Theodora, was smiling to himself. He was feeling, suddenly, ridiculously happy. It was suddenly quite clear to him that his beloved, for reasons he was as yet unable to guess at, had allowed herself to be entangled in an engagement that neither she, nor his ward, had any intention of fulfilling.

Looking back at the night of their engagement party, he wondered that he had not realised the truth then, but knew that he had been blinded by his own jealousy. Knowing Theodora, he thought it had been her own idea from the beginning. Why she should be looking so careworn was quite another matter, however, and he was determined not to let her out of his sight, sure that her uncharacteristic withdrawal from the party had some ulterior aim.

Concealing himself, without too much difficulty, in a place where he could see her without being observed, he set himself to watch. He did not have long to wait. Theodora, rising from the rustic bench where she had been resting, stole to the edge of the trees, and spent a few seconds regarding the throngs disporting themselves in the garden. Apparently reassured, she came back, and made her way along a path which led, he knew, to the stables. Prudently withdrawing behind a large tree-trunk, he waited until the sound of her slippered feet, almost but not quite silent on the soft grass, had passed by, and gone some way ahead. Waiting until he was sure she was indeed making for the stables, he then took himself off by another route.

His only difficulty was that he could not appear there until he could be sure she had gone. He was fairly sure that she was generally as aware of his presence as he was of hers, and he had not missed the fact that she had been looking for him earlier, though he had done his best, out of pique, to stay out of her sight. Now, one glimpse of his unmistakable height and colouring would be enough. He waited, therefore, out of the way, and was rewarded by a glimpse of Lady Lingdale's carriage, driven by a coachman who had, with extreme reluctance, torn himself from the generous hospitality offered to all the visiting servants. She was sitting well back, to be out of the sight of any chance passer-by, but he knew that she must be inside. At once he made his way to the yard, and demanded a horse.

The groom looked at him in horror.

"A horse! But sir . . . !"

"Saddle me a horse, damn you, and be quick about it!"

"But sir, your clothes! You're not dressed for riding! They'll be ruined!"

It was true. His black silk breeches and white silk stockings were far from being suitable equestrian wear, but he was in no mood to worry.

"I'll be the judge of that. Will you saddle me a horse, or must I do it myself?"

"Yes, sir. Right away, sir." The groom knew better than to argue with a man who was, as well as being a frequent visitor, also known to be generous with his gifts to servants.

"Stay a moment! That carriage which has just left, where was it going?"

A gleam of comprehension shone in the groom's mind, though he had more sense than to allow any sign of it to appear on his face.

"The young lady, sir? She was wanting to go to Mr. Bellerby's house. She visited there once before, when she was staying here, and her Highness sent her in one of our own chaises. She had us give directions to her coachman."

"Excellent. Be so good as to repeat the directions to me."

The groom looked doubtful, but the sight of a gleam of gold casually displayed in Mr. Ravensworth's hand was enough to allay his qualms. The directions given, and the horse saddled and brought, Ravensworth swung himself up into the saddle, and without more ado set off in pursuit of his maddening, headstrong love.

CHAPTER TWELVE

THE HOUSE WAS JUST as Theodora had remembered it from her previous visit. Surrounded as it was by laurels and other evergreen trees, even the fresh green of new leaves was absent, and last year's tarnished foliage, blown from neighbouring woodland, still lay in decaying heaps and drifts, stifling the growth of all but the rankest grass and weeds. One would have thought it a house long deserted, empty for many years. Theodora, who had brought only the coachman and no other servant, told him to stay with his horses, and herself went to the door. The steps, slippery with green algae even in this warm, dry weather, looked as if they had not been trodden by human foot for months, if not years.

There was no knocker on the door, and she beat on it with her fists. The sound she made seemed so weak that she could not believe that anyone would hear it, in a house that seemed all but devoid of servants. Looking around, she spied a length of branch that had fallen on to the drive, and went back to pick it up. With this she was able to make a more satisfactory noise. No one came for what seemed like an age, and she was lifting her piece of wood to repeat her assault when the door slowly opened.

The elderly servant, whom she had seen before, started back at the sight of the stick in her hand, and inadvertently swung the door wider.

"Good day," said Theodora with what coolness she could muster. "I am Miss Waverton. You may remember I visited here once before."

The man stared at her in horror. He said nothing, but stood holding the door as if it was the only thing that kept him from falling over, which perhaps it was. Theodora decided to interpret this as an invitation to enter, and stepped over the threshold, unwittingly bringing her stick with her. She had almost forgotten that she was holding it, but there was perhaps some subconscious need for its solid reassurance that made her continue to clasp it.

"I should like to see your master," declared Theodora in a louder voice, since it occurred to her that he was possibly hard of hearing. This information took a few moments to sink in, and provoked no more than a long, slow shake of the head.

"You do not mean to tell me that he is not here? I thought he never went anywhere."

Again the silent negative, which could have meant almost anything, Theodora thought. She began to wonder whether the man was a simpleton, or in his dotage.

"Is there no other servant here?" She looked around. His head shake came with more alacrity now, and a minute gleam that might have been wakening intelligence shone in his rheumy eyes.

"You do not mean to tell me that you are the only one? And you care for your master, and the house, and do the cooking too?" Looking round her, she thought that it was more than likely, and was glad that at no time had she ever been offered refreshments in this place. "No, you do not mean to tell me anything at all, do you? Then kindly take me to your master."

The movement of his head was even more definite, and there was a look in his eyes that could have been fear. She had a momentary vision of what life must be like for this man, grown old, probably, in his master's service. He was obviously lacking in intelligence, to say the least, or else he would never have stayed in this dismal place, with a man whom he feared. Forcing herself to disregard the unwholesome greasy dirtiness of his clothes and person, and the rank, almost animal smell that emanated from them, she drew nearer and laid a hand on his arm. He shrank away, but, when he saw that it was a caress rather than a blow, looked into her face with amazement and a dawning gleam of gratitude. She was touched, and spoke gently to him.

"You do not want to, do you? But I think you must. See, I have had a letter from Mr. Bellerby." She laid down her stick, which movement occasioned a slight relaxation in the old man's stance. "Come, you did not think I was going to attack you, did you? What very odd ideas you must have about young women, to be sure! Now, I am certain I brought that letter with me."

With both her hands free, she ferreted in her reticule, in which she had prudently put both of the letters she had received from her great-uncle, and withdrew the first of the two, commanding her presence, and keeping her fingers over the date. He would have taken it, but she whisked it out of his reach.

"No, you may look at it just as well from there, and see that it is indeed in your master's hand. If you are his only servant, you must have attended to sending it off?" His thoughtful stillness showed that her guess was correct; she could only hope that he was not privy to his master's correspondence, or he would know that this was not the recent letter.

Head on one side like an aged bird confronting a large and lively worm, the old man peered at the letter. He was still shaking his head, but more, she thought, from habit than anything else. When he had finished looking at it, he raised his eyes to her face again.

"So you see? I think you had better do as I say."

Still he hesitated, and the thin thread of Theodora's patience, already frayed by anxiety, snapped.

"Well, if you will not do so, I suppose I must find my own way. It should not be so very difficult." Scarcely aware of what she did, she picked up her stick, which she had leaned against the wall, and firmly made her way across the hall the way she had gone before. With a twitter of dismay the old servant, abandoning the door at last and leaving it still ajar, came after her with a swift, crablike shuffle. For a moment she thought he meant to head her off, but she soon saw that her decisive action had made him give in. With an air of resignation he passed her, and led her through the same maze of corridors and rooms until she was in front of the doors she remembered from before. There he hung back, unwilling to be the one to brave the possible wrath. Nothing loath, Theodora opened the door and went in.

Mr. Bellerby must, she supposed, have risen from his chair during the intervening weeks, but it was hard not to think that he had simply remained there, gathering dust in the dank silence of the room, since her last visit.

"Who's there? Who's that? Don't come any nearer! I am armed, you know!"

Indeed, as her eyes grew accustomed to the gloom which seemed unabated by the brightness of the May sunshine outside, Theodora saw a glint of light in the chair, and perceived that it came from a pistol barrel that was pointing, somewhat unsteadily, in her direction. Standing very still, she fixed her look above it, finding the gleam of those dark eyes that must be able to see her, in her white dress, better than she could see him. The pistol did not waver.

"It is I, Theodora Waverton," she said with slow clarity. "You must remember me. I was here before, at your invitation, and you have written to me only the other day."

"Written to you, yes! But not invited you here!" Behind her Theodora felt, rather than heard, a flutter of apprehension as the manservant's worst fears were realised.

"Where's that man of mine? Did he let you in? Sim! Where are you, Sim?" With extreme reluctance the servant shuffled into the room, keeping half behind Theodora and seeming to shrink his already bowed form into a smaller compass. "What were you thinking of, allowing this hussy to bother me? Get rid of her at once!"

"You need not blame him," said Theodora, feeling rather sorry for the old man. "He certainly did not let me in at all willingly. In fact, I forced him to!"

"Forced him to? Bribed him, more like."

"Not at all. I threatened him with a stick," she said resourcefully, brandishing her erstwhile door-knocker, and forgetting for a moment the pistol that he held.

"Threatened him? That's armed trespass, that is! If not breaking and entering! Call for help, Sim!"

"Don't be silly," she retorted with some impatience. "I know very well there is no one to call, except my coachman, and what good will he do? By the time Sim had found anyone, I would be long gone, if I were really a miscreant. As it is, you cannot imagine with what reluctance you find me here. Wild horses wouldn't have dragged me, if it had not seemed so important."

An unseen and unknown-of audience, quietly stationed round the corner of the corridor, smiled his appreciation. Ravensworth had arrived not very long after she had gone into the house, and had wasted no time in following her. Tossing the reins of his horse to the surprised coachman, who looked as though he was longing to ask what was going on but had not the nerve to do so, he had stridden up the steps, his lip curling in disgust at the state of the house. Finding the front door still ajar, he had wasted no time in knocking, but simply walked in, and made his way quietly through the house. It had taken him a few minutes to find out her whereabouts, but the sound of those clear tones had led him unerringly to her.

Satisfied that she was safe and in control of the situation, he set himself to listen and learn. Jonas Bellerby he knew only by repute, but the man had not a very pleasant reputation, and, while he would back his Theodora against most adversaries, this one had maybe more power than most to upset her.

"I'll have the law on you," Bellerby was muttering viciously.

"Well, you are welcome to try, but I should think you would make yourself a laughing-stock," responded Theodora judiciously. "After all, the Princess herself knows that you invited me here once, and you will hardly care to admit that a girl of eighteen, with no more than a piece of rotten wood, was able to threaten her way into your presence. Besides, my coachman himself is witness to the fact that your man opened the door to me, and I entered without difficulty. In any case, surely all this is beside the point? I am here now, by whatever means. Will you let me speak? I give you my word, I mean no harm to you."

There was a short silence. Ravensworth guessed that Bellerby did not really believe that Theodora meant him any harm. He was simply unaccustomed to having anyone visit him, and naturally suspicious, fearing as all misers did that he might lose some of his precious possessions. Nevertheless, this was no stranger, and he had written to her quite recently.

"Very well," was the grudging answer. "But set aside that club, at least. I suppose you had better sit down. You'll be wanting to polish the chair again, no doubt, like last time. A simple print gown, like your mother wore at your age, would be more practical than that silk you're decked out in, my girl, and would wash a sight better!"

"No doubt," replied Theodora with composure. "It would scarcely be a compliment to the Princess, however. Today is her birthday, as you must surely know, and I am invited to Oatlands to help celebrate it. I took the opportunity, since I was so near, to visit you."

"Ay, mighty civil of you! No doubt you want something! You'd not come else."

"For the pleasure of your conversation? No," she said reflectively, "I wouldn't. Now you are quite sure I am not going to attack you, will you not let Sim get back to his duties? I am sure there must be some little task he could be getting on with. Like cleaning the house, for instance?"

Ravensworth grinned again, and sent up a silent cheer, before looking around him for a hiding place. Easing open a nearby door, he found an empty closet and slipped inside, leaving the door ajar. His caution was unnecessary.

"Don't you go off, Sim! I'm not having her here alone with me! You shall be my witness, so mind you listen to what she says!"

"Oh, can he speak, then?" asked Theodora artlessly. "Or will he be obliged to write it all? Poor man, perhaps he had better take notes."

"He can speak well enough when he wants. But I've taught him to hold his tongue. I've no use for endless gibble-gabble. So say what you've come to say, miss, and have done. You'd best be back to that grand party of yours."

"Very well. I have come to tell you that I am not going to marry Lord Lingdale."

"So you've seen sense at last, have you? I thought you would, when you knew I was serious about leaving you my money."

She sighed.

"I do wish you would forget about your wretched money! That has nothing to do with it!"

He was silently disbelieving.

"What I mean is, that I never was going to marry Lord Lingdale. He does not want it, and nor do I. It is merely a ruse, for a while."

"And the reason for this ruse?"

Theodora was less than comfortable about this, and tried to cover it with little success.

"That is private—a matter between the two of us that need not concern you."

"But I think it does. I think it concerns me very closely! I was right, was I not, that the young man is in debt?"

Theodora could not deny it, but she tightened her lips on giving an untrue answer.

"I thought so. In fact, I know so. He has been gambling, I suppose, and has lost more money than he can afford. Not that that would be so great an amount, for the young man has a very indifferent fortune, I hear, though his guardian is so rich. The guardian, now, there's the man for you! Set your cap at him, my girl, and I'll leave you every last groat!"

"I would not set my cap at him, as you so vulgarly term it, if he were the last man in London!" Theodora retorted, stung out of her silence. "And anyway, he doesn't like me," she finished more moderately. Ravensworth, listening with complete concentration, was all attention. The servant Sim, who had long since lost all understanding of the exchange, slowly scratched at his balding head and allowed his eyes to glaze over. Long practice had taught him to take his repose when and where he might, even standing up.

"Don't try and change the subject," ordered Mr. Bellerby unfairly.

"I wasn't! It was you!"

"And don't contradict me. I say that young Lord of yours has been losing money at cards, and don't know how to pay it back. Why not ask that guardian of his? He could find it ten times over, and not notice the loss."

"I know. I did suggest it, but he wouldn't," admitted Theodora, finding herself for the first time in accord with her unpleasant relative. "Mr. Ravensworth has been rather stern, in the past, and I'm afraid Edmund is a little frightened of him. Besides, he might refuse."

"And let his ward be taken up for debt? Not a chance. A coward, then, hiding behind your skirts and my money."

"He is not!" Theodora flew to Edmund's defence. "I can *quite* understand why he did not choose to ask Mr. Ravensworth. And I felt I must help him! Why not, when it cost me nothing, and was so easy?"

"Cost you nothing? How are you intending to break it off, without being branded either a flirt, or a woman cast off by her lover? And when is this event to take place? Not until he has found the money to repay his debt, and that won't be for a year or two, I can assure you!"

This, the flaw in the whole plan, was what Theodora herself had been worrying about, and it did not help to have it thus spelled out to her.

"Well, I don't know precisely how we should do it, but I am certain nothing could be simpler. We are sure to think of something. And why should it be so long before Edmund has paid off his debt?"

"Surely you know the size of it, girl?"

"Yes, I do, but—"

"Five thousand pounds," Bellerby said, relishing the words as if they were some delicious titbit. "Five thousand pounds, to say nothing of the interest he must pay on it. He'll be lucky to find a quarter of that before he comes of age in two years time, unless he wins it at the table. And you should know by now that he's more likely to lose more than to win, that way."

Theodora stared at him in horror.

"How did you know...?" she whispered.

"The amount? That's just it, my girl. You thought that I, living out here all alone, would not hear of what's going on, but that's where you're wrong. I have, you see, a certain—shall we say—arrangement, of a profitable financial nature, with several gentlemen in the city. Money is no use unless it is working, my dear! So I put my money to work, and very handsomely it rewards me, too."

"I don't understand you."

"Such an innocent! Where do you think the money comes from that those good, kind gentlemen lend to young fools like your Lingdale, when they get themselves into difficulties? From the top of a magic beanstalk? No, my dear, it comes from me, and others like me. And it just so happens, my dear, that the good, kind gentleman who was so generous as to lend the sum I have already mentioned to a young Lord of our acquaintance was by way of being an associate of mine. So when he heard that the surety offered was marriage with yourself, and my fortune coming to you, he pricked up his ears. He lent the money, yes, but he pretty soon let me know what was in the wind. Now do you see, or shall I draw you a picture?"

Theodora sat, dumb and frozen, in her chair. It was like some kind of horrible nightmare, and the old man's words were spinning a web round her to entrap her, while he sat in the centre like the old spider he was, ready to suck her dry. The feeling was so strong that she looked down at her hands, stretching them and clasping them together, as if to make sure that she could still move, that the sticky threads had not immobilised her.

"So, you are Shylock after all," she said softly, not looking at him.

"I am not ashamed to own it. In all but the religion, of course, I am."

"And you want your pound of flesh." It was a statement, not a question.

"Only a pound? Oh, no, my dear. I want much more than that. I want you."

She looked at him in horror, and he laughed. Ravensworth flung open the door of his closet, and stepped out. This had gone far enough.

"No need to look at me like that, girl! It is not as a woman that I want you—I am too old, and women have never interested me much anyway. Nothing has, really, except money. My money is my wife, my child, my everything. I want it to come to you, because you have spirit, and are not a fool, though you may behave like one at times. It shall all be yours, but you must bind yourself to do my will."

"I will not! I cannot!"

"You must." His voice, suddenly powerful, was implacable. "Otherwise the debt will be called in, and your young Edmund will be ruined. Oh, I don't doubt you do not mean to marry him, but you must be fond of him, to enter into something like this in the first place. Don't try to tell me it wasn't all your idea, for I won't believe you. By all accounts, he's neither the brains nor the audacity for it.

"But you have, my dear, you have! And, between us, we might rule the country! The Regent is a fool, always was and always will be, spending his money on houses and paintings and childish toys like that. With my money, and your looks…he's married, I know, but all the world knows they detest one another. Oh, he'd not be able to resist the allure of all that gold!"

He was almost raving.

"You—you would make me his mistress?" Theodora gave an hysterical giggle. "But all the world knows he only falls in love with grandmothers! You are raving!"

"I think he would discount the trifling disadvantage of your age, for the sake of the money. He is desperately in debt again, you know."

"You are mad," said Theodora, rising to her feet. "I will not stay to hear any more of this. I had thought to beg you, to plead with you, for Edmund's sake, but I see that it is no use. I will never see you again."

"You'll not leave yet!" Ravensworth, outside the door, had hesitated just too long. Theodora stayed frozen to the spot as the old man rose to his feet, his rugs falling in a heap around him. In his hand the small black eye of the pistol, steady for once, stared at her. "You will not go until I give you leave, and I have not done so."

There was a mad light in that black, unblinking regard. Sim, roused out of his torpor, gave a whimper, but was ignored. Ravensworth, whose hand was on the door, stood motionless, and cursed the fact that his formal attire meant that he was completely unarmed.

Theodora stared back at him.

"I will never do what you want," she said flatly. "I will never marry, or give myself, to please you. I will never accept a penny of your money. Rather than that, I would choose death."

She walked towards him, and the gun wavered. A look of doubt crossed the old man's face, and his other hand came up to fumble with the limp, greyish neckcloth that he wore. He gave a sudden, wordless cry, and dropped the pistol, the bullet smashing the window. The tinkle of falling glass was ignored by them all, as the old man raised both hands to claw at his neck, his chest, then crumpled like an unmanned puppet on to the pool of rugs at his feet.

Ravensworth burst through the door, fearing to find Theodora wounded or worse, but instead she was on her knees at her great-uncle's side. The manservant crouched against the wall, both hands before his face, and moaning. Small as she was, Bellerby's thin body, dried out like the brittle corpse of some long-dead bird, was no difficulty for her to move, and she eased him out straight, pulling down the hands that still clutched at his breast. Ripping open his shirt, she laid her hand on his chest, then again his neck. His face was shocked, surprised, the eyes staring, the mouth already slack.

Theodora sat back on her knees, her hands falling helplessly to her side. Ravensworth took a step forward, and she looked back at him. She showed no surprise or pleasure at his appearance—one great shock had driven all lesser ones out of her head.

"My dear, my darling!" he exclaimed, starting forward as she rose to her feet, swaying. She let him support her, but held him off when he would have held her close.

"Oh, Ravensworth, he is dead, and I have killed him," she said, very low. He leaned down, in his turn, and put his hand to feel that stilled pulse. He gave a reluctant nod. Then her face crumpled like a child's, and at once he swept her up into his arms and carried her to the window, his feet crunching unheeded over the broken glass. It was a casement, so deep as to be almost a French window, securely bolted and fastened, but with the key in the lock.

Setting Theodora down, still holding her close in his comforting grasp, he undid bolts and turned the key, then shook the window until, hinges complaining, it opened. Then, without more ado he lifted her again, and stepped over the low sill and out into the fresh, clean air. She lay passive on his breast, neither sobbing nor speaking, the tears running unheeded down her white cheeks.

Ravensworth found himself on the remains of a paved terrace, though the old stones had all but disappeared under a carpet of encroaching weeds, and the wistaria that cloaked the walls had sent out long, trailing stems that formed a mat, fringed now with new pinkish leaves. The flowers were no more than fat, silvery tassels, but a few more days of sunshine would open them to fragrant, luscious beauty. Picking his way, fearful of catching his foot in one of those ropelike branches, he made his way to a stone seat. Careless for once of his clothes, he brushed off a mat of leaves and twigs, and sat on it, with Theodora curled on his knee. She was shaking now, and he gentled her as he would have a horse.

Finally the trembling subsided, and he felt an almost imperceptible movement of withdrawal. He allowed his own grip to slacken, so that she might easily free herself from his embrace if she chose.

"He is dead, and I killed him," she repeated tonelessly.

Unperceived, the elderly Sim had followed them. He hovered in the shadow of an overhanging curtain of wistaria. His voice seemed to creak with disuse.

"Oh, no, miss. Not you. It was him, you see. Knew he had a bad heart, he did. Took bad with it before, twice, getting in a rage with me. He always had a shocking temper, when he didn't get his own way," he finished, with some pride. Theodora turned her head to look at him; it was as if a statue had spoken to her.

"Why, I've never heard you speak! You saw it, didn't you? That pistol was loaded!"

"It certainly was," put in Ravensworth, and his arms unconsciously tightened round her. "You could have been killed."

"And don't think he wouldn't have done it, miss. It was his own wickedness that killed him, in the end."

"But what are we to do? We cannot hide that I was here, and there is sure to be talk! And Edmund, poor Edmund, what of him?"

"To hell with Edmund," said Edmund's guardian brutally. For the first time Theodora looked up into his face, and seemed suddenly to realise the impropriety of her position. A glow of colour stained her cheeks, and she would have started up, but Ravensworth's arms held her as if they had been iron bars, and his hazel eyes burned into hers.

"Let me go!" she said breathlessly.

"I will—if you really want me to," he responded. "Is that truly what you would like, my darling?"

Her mind said "yes," but her traitorous lips had just time to shape the word "no" before he silenced her with a kiss. Under the interested gaze of Sim, who was seeing more adventure that day than he had done in all his life, the kiss continued for a long time. When at last Ravensworth raised his head, her eyes were languorous, the pupils dilated as if she had put belladonna into them. Her lips, no longer pale, curved up into a tentative smile, and she shyly raised one hand to his cheek. He turned his face to put a kiss into her palm.

"I have never felt skin like that before," she said wonderingly, "so smooth one way, and rough the other."

"Not too rough, I hope?" His eyes were laughing at her.

"Oh, no! I like it!" she said happily. "Must you shave it every day? May I watch?"

He could not restrain his laughter, and she had to join him, though she did not mean to.

"Do not laugh at me! Remember, I never had a father that I knew of." She was immediately sober again, reminded of the silent figure in the room nearby. "Oh, how shocking; I had actually forgotten him." She looked around, and saw Sim still standing, watching them. "Well, really, Ravensworth, I did not know we had an audience.

You might have sent him away, for you can see he has not thought to go!"

"Not at all. He is your chaperon," replied he, kissing her again.

"But, Ravensworth..."

"Don't worry, he wasn't shocked last time. I don't suppose he will be this time, either." He kissed her ruthlessly, and she subsided into his embrace, both unable and unwilling to resist him.

CHAPTER THIRTEEN

AT LAST, albeit unwillingly, Theodora set her hands against Ravensworth's chest, and pushed him away.

"We must think what we are to do! Time is passing, and we shall both be missed."

"Don't worry. I have it all worked out," he soothed her. She did not know whether to be amused or insulted. He looked at her, and correctly interpreted her look.

"My mind works best when it is—er—stimulated," he said audaciously, and she stifled a giggle. "Now, the first thing we have to do is to get the old man into his bed. It will not matter what we say, if he is found in there with the pistol at his side and broken glass all over the floor. His servant and I will go and do this at once, and you must remain here. You will not mind?"

She braced herself to smile for him.

"No. I can help you, if you want. I have seen death before, in the village, and I am not afraid."

He looked at her sternly.

"You will have nothing to do with it while I am here to protect you. Just stay here, in the sun. We will not be long."

Thoughtfully, he took off his coat and spread it on the stone seat, so that her white dress should not be marked. She watched him, towering tall over the bent figure of the old servant, as they walked back to the broken window, and heard once again the scrunch of their feet on the broken glass. Then there was silence, and she resolutely turned her mind away from what they must do, carrying that slight body to some bedchamber, undressing it, and putting it into a suitable nightshirt, ready for the doctors and, later, the undertaker's men to see it.

Theodora closed her eyes, and lifted her face to the sun. It glowed fiery through her eyelids, and the soft warmth of May, lacking the fierce bite of full summer, caressed her skin. The shocks of the previous hour took their toll, and a merciful oblivion overtook her so that, though she did not sleep, she was scarcely aware of the passage of time. At last the red gold warmth on her eyes was dimmed to black, and she returned from whatever limbo her mind had wandered to.

Ravensworth stood before her, looking rather grim. She looked at him anxiously.

"What is it? Has anything gone wrong?"

His expression lightened.

"No. I could not help remembering how close you were to death by that old madman."

"Oh, hush. He was mad, as you say, but he did me no harm. And I am free of him now."

He took her hands, and pulled her to her feet. Holding her close, he rested his cheek on the top of her head.

"You must go back now. Back to Oatlands, I mean, and then home to Amelia Lingdale, and Edmund with you. I must stay here and see the doctor, when he comes."

"Am I to hide my visit here? I am not sure it can be done; the grooms at the stables know about it, at least."

"No, it cannot be hidden. You will say that you received a summons from your great-uncle, who felt himself to be unwell. You came here at all speed, but arrived only just in time to see him breathe his last."

"But what about you? Why did you come?"

"To ask for your hand, of course! I had been concealing a secret passion—well, I have, you know!—and wished to gain Mr. Bellerby's consent."

"They will say you were after his fortune," she said shrewdly.

"Let them. It will soon be seen to be no such thing, and besides, without wishing to boast, I am quite wealthy enough already. I have no need of a rich bride."

"But what about Edmund? I am engaged to him, don't forget."

"I have not forgotten. Wretched boy!"

"You must not be too angry with him," she pleaded anxiously. "He is a little afraid of you, you know."

"And so he should be. The young fool, getting himself into debt and allowing you to help him out of it in this way. Why did he not come to me?"

She said nothing, but looked at him. After a moment he gave a little frown.

"Well, I suppose you are right. I did not mean to be hard on the boy, you know. I suppose I took my responsibilities too seriously, at times, and tried to take his father's place, when I was too young to do so. I meant it for the best."

"I know. And I think he does, too, when he stops to consider. But he has his pride, too, and to be coming to you to ask for money, for such a reason, was more than he could do. You cannot blame me for wanting to help him."

"I can, but I will not. Now you must go. I shall see you later, when all of this is dealt with. Tell Edmund what you will; he must leave the party and escort you home, for of course it is not to be thought of that you should be dancing now. Tell him I am sorry he will have to miss the fireworks."

He gave her one last hard kiss, then sent her back to her carriage in charge of Sim, by a route that avoided the room where Jonas Bellerby had died. The old man was as silent as before, and when they reached the entrance hall she stopped and turned to him.

"Do not worry about your future," she said kindly. "I will do my best to see that you are cared for, now that your master is gone."

He gave an awkward, nodding bow, like an owl hunching its body.

"He weren't what you could call a good master," he said in his slow, creaking voice, "but I were used to him." It was not much of a tribute, but she was obscurely glad to know that someone, for some reason, would miss the old miser.

At Oatlands Park she was not surprised to find that her absence had passed unnoticed. Familiar with the house, she was able to find a small, empty sitting-room, and sent an obliging servant to find Edmund and bring him to her. He arrived, rather annoyed at being summoned from the entertainments, and aghast when he saw her, for in spite of her care the fine white tiffany of her gown was dirty and stained, and her face still retained traces of the ordeal she had passed.

"Dora! Whatever has happened? You look terrible!"

"Yes, thank you, Edmund."

"I didn't mean . . . that is, you know—"

"Never mind, Edmund. It doesn't matter now. I have a great deal to tell you, but first I am afraid we must go home. At once."

"Now? But the party is hardly begun! Surely you can contrive to tidy up your gown, and, with evening coming, no one will notice if it is a bit dirty. At nine o'clock the Duchess is to lead off the dancing, and then there are the fireworks! You would not want to miss them, would you?"

Theodora could scarcely restrain a smile.

"Yes. Mr. Ravensworth thought you would not want to miss that. He asked me to tell you he was sorry about them."

"Cousin Alexander? What has he to do with all this? What have you been doing, Theodora?"

She saw that it had been a mistake to mention his guardian's name, for he was looking truculent, and his voice was getting louder than she liked. Going to him, she put a pleading hand on his arm, and spoke softly.

"Pray, Edmund, do not speak so loud! I have done nothing that should displease you, and indeed I have had a very uncomfortable afternoon, on your behalf. If it were not for Mr. Ravensworth, I might well have been in serious difficulties. But I *cannot* speak of it here, where anyone may hear us. I have to tell you, though, that my great-uncle is dead, and because of that I must go home at once. Please take me back!" The tears rose unbidden to her eyes, and at once he capitulated.

"Oh, yes, of course, Dora, only please do not cry!" he begged in some alarm. "We will go straight away, naturally. So the old man is dead, is he? I knew he was old, of course, but I never expected...however, you will not wish to be talking of that now. Just leave everything to me, and I will call for the carriage at once."

"Thank you, Edmund. It is such a relief to be able to rely on you," she replied meekly, and allowed him to bustle about, sending messages of apology to their hostess, and commanding the carriage to be brought round straight away.

On the journey home, safe in the privacy of the carriage, she tackled the difficult task of telling him what had happened. It was not possible, of course, to tell Edmund the tale that Ravensworth had thought up, so she produced her great-uncle's letter, and handed it to him. He read it through, and turned horrified eyes on her.

"This is terrible! When did you receive it?"

"I forget. About two days ago."

"And did not tell me? You poor girl, why ever not? You do not think I would permit you to lose your inheritance for my sake, do you? What a poor thing you must think me."

Touched by his concern, and by the fact that his first thought was obviously for her, she put her hand on his.

"My dear Edmund, you must believe me when I tell you that I have never wanted his fortune—indeed, nothing would induce me to accept it! I was only worried that he might ruin you. I think he would have done it, too, for he is . . . was . . . a horrid old man."

"Oh, hush! Did you not say he is dead?"

"Yes, but I don't see how that changes things. He *was* a horrid old man, Edmund, and, what is more, I believe it was his own temper killed him! He was so angry, you see, when I told him that . . . when I disagreed with him, that he had a heart attack!"

Edmund was rather inclined to be shocked by her attitude, for, in spite of his poetical aspirations, he was at heart the soul of convention. He reminded himself, however, that she was no doubt in a state of shock after so frightening an occurrence, and made allowances.

"Poor Dora," he said with sympathy. "I would not have had you go through such an ordeal, on my behalf, for the world! Did he die at once?"

"Yes, and it was very fortunate that he did," remarked his betrothed, "for otherwise he might have shot me."

She spoke prosaically, and Edmund stared at her, clearly prey to the fear that her mind had been unhinged by the events of the afternoon.

"It is quite true, you know! Ravensworth will tell you, for he heard it all. He was outside the door, but he was powerless to help me, for the pistol was pointing directly at me. I was very frightened, for of course I did not know that he was there, and, though I hoped that the pistol might not be loaded, one could not be sure of it. And, of course, it was."

"It was what?" His brain seemed to have turned numb, and he could scarcely follow what she said.

"Loaded. He dropped it, when he felt the heart attack starting, and it went off. Luckily, it only broke the window. And then Ravensworth burst in, but by that time Mr. Bellerby was already dead."

Edmund's mind seized on the name as a point of sanity in what otherwise seemed to him like the ravings of a lunatic.

"Cousin Alexander? What was he doing there, anyway?"

"Well, he had seen me leave, and learned that I was visiting my great-uncle." She turned away her face so that Edmund should not see the rising colour in her cheeks. Fortunately, that young man was so accustomed to finding his guardian taking an interest or, as his ward would term it, interfering, in his affairs, that he did not question why Mr. Ravensworth should find it necessary to do such a thing. Theodora felt that Edmund had received enough shocks, for a while without finding that his supposed fiancée was in love with his guardian. Overwrought as she already felt herself to be, she could not bear the incredulity, not to say the horror, he would undoubtedly display on hearing of it. Besides, in the eyes of the world she was betrothed to him. In the eyes of the world and, more particularly, in the eyes of his mama.

"Listen, Edmund, for we are nearly home, and we must think what we are to say to your mother," she said urgently. This aspect of things had not hitherto occurred to him. His face became, if possible, even more alarmed than before.

"Yes, of course! What are we to say?"

Swiftly Theodora outlined the story that Ravensworth had suggested, repeating it until she was sure that Edmund had it by heart. It would be useless to attempt to hide Ravensworth's presence at Mr. Bellerby's house, since he intended to stay until the doctor arrived, and they settled that Theodora had asked him to be present, as Edmund's guardian. She hoped that Lady Amelia would accept this.

"I am afraid, Edmund, that I shall have to tell her that I will not be my great-uncle's heiress. It would be unkind to her to let her think that I am, for the disappointment would be even greater when the truth were told."

Edmund looked thoughtful.

"She won't like it, you know. She's got her heart set on my marrying an heiress. Not that she isn't fond of you, you know that, Dora, but she won't like our engagement so well when she knows you have no fortune."

"Then that will give us a good reason to bring it to an end."

He continued to look as dubious as he felt. He hardly liked to mention his own problems, but he could not help remembering that his debt had still to be paid. He realised, with a shock, that, whether or not his engagement continued, he himself was in difficulties, for news that Theodora would inherit nothing would soon reach the ears of the moneylenders. Theodora was not slow to interpret his silence.

"I should perhaps tell you, Edmund, that your guardian knows all about the money you borrowed," she said in a small voice. "Do not be angry with me; he heard me talking to Mr. Bellerby about it, and I was obliged to tell him the whole. And the most dreadful part is that Mr. Bellerby—I cannot think of him as my great-uncle—was the one who lent the money to you! It seems he had a business arrangement with the people you went to, and it was his money that they were lending at interest, on his behalf! That is how he came to hear of your using his name."

Edmund was appalled. For two pins he would have stopped the carriage and gone, he knew not where—abroad, perhaps—and never shown his face to his family again. Only his sense of his duty to care for Theodora prevented him.

"I expect Ravensworth was very angry," he said with a fair attempt at calmness.

"He was, rather," was the chilling reply. Then Theodora caught sight of his expression. "Oh, not with you! At least, not really. Of course, he does not like it that you should have such a debt, but I think he is angry with himself that you had not felt yourself able to ask for his help. Do not worry, Edmund! I think you will find him much more understanding than you thought. Oh, here we are already! I quite dread telling your mother, Edmund! She has been so kind to me, and now to disappoint her like this! It is too bad!"

Edmund pulled himself together.

"Don't worry about it, Dora. I shall tell her myself." He handed Theodora down from the carriage, and took her solicitously indoors. Lady Lingdale, alarmed by their return from the first great event of the Season at so extraordinary an hour, was in the hall to greet them, and at first could think of nothing but her relief at finding that they were neither of them ill. Edmund shepherded his two ladies back to the drawing-room, and proceeded to break to his mother the news that Mr. Bellerby was dead. A dawning excitement on her face made him continue, very quickly, wih the news that Theodora would not be inheriting his fortune.

"Not? But why, then, did he send for you?"

This reasonable question silenced Edmund completely, and he turned wild eyes to Theodora, who rose and came to Lady Lingdale, seating herself beside her.

"What Edmund should have said, ma'am, is that, even if Mr. Bellerby should leave all his fortune to me, I will not accept it."

"Not accept it? My dear child, you are raving! This has all been too much for you; you should take some of my restorative drops, and go to bed. You will feel much better in the morning."

"It is kind of you, dear Lady Lingdale," said Theodora, taking the older woman's hand to prevent her ringing for the servants. "I am not much upset, however—at least, not by his death. I do most sincerely mean what I say. If you knew how he treated Mama, and his behaviour to me, you would not expect me to take his money."

"But Theodora!" Lady Lingdale's voice rose to a wail. "What about Edmund?"

"I did not get engaged to Theodora merely because she was an heiress!" interpolated Edmund indignantly, quite forgetting that he had done exactly that.

"No, of course not! But you must see, dearest, that it does make a difference!"

"Of course it does," Theodora interrupted quickly, for she could see that her erstwhile suitor was seething with annoyance that his mother should impute such mercenary motives to him. "In fact, Edmund and I have agreed that we should part. Haven't we, Edmund?"

"Oh, yes," he agreed sullenly in response to her gimlet look.

"Impossible!" exclaimed Lady Lingdale. "It is not to be thought of!"

The two young people stared at her in surprise.

"You know, Mama, I do not think we should suit," pointed out Edmund. "We have agreed that we would not be happy together and, even if Dora had been an heiress, we should not have married.''

''Maybe. I know nothing of that. All I know is, if you call it off now, everyone will say that you were only marrying her for her money, and that now she hasn't any, you are casting her off!''

''But if we tell them—'' attempted Theodora.

''Oh, you may tell people whatever you like, but that will not stop them thinking! They will say that you are cruel and heartless, and me too, most likely! I will not stand for it!'' Overwrought, Lady Lingdale shed tears, while her son and Theodora exchanged anxious glances. ''And to think, only an hour ago, I was so happy!''

Theodora attempted to comfort her, but was repulsed. ''Wretched girl! This is all your fault! You entrapped him into marriage, pretending that you would be an heiress, and now you say you will not accept the money! I never heard anything so unnatural!''

Edmund rose to his feet.

''Now, Mama, I will not permit you to talk to Dora like that,'' he said in firm tones that his mother had never heard him use to her before. ''If anyone is to blame for all this, it is I.''

''You? How can you say so, my poor deceived boy?''

''I have not been deceived, and I will not have you say so. Theodora's behaviour has been above reproach. Whatever happens, we must see that no slur attaches to her name, and I forbid you to say anything that might hurt her!''

Lady Lingdale stared up at this new, masterful son, impressed in spite of herself. Never before had he spoken to her in such a tone, and for the first time in his life Edmund reminded her of his father, whose word to her had been law.

"Bravo, Edmund!" said Ravensworth, who had entered unannounced and had not been noticed. "Very well said! I always knew you had it in you!"

Edmund turned and looked his guardian in the eye. He felt a surge of courage, for that cold, sarcastic look that he had always feared was quite absent.

"Ravensworth! What on earth are you doing here?" Lady Lingdale found her tongue again.

"I think Edmund told you, ma'am, that he came to Mr. Bellerby's house to help me, and stayed to speak to the doctor," explained Theodora, who found herself unable to look at Ravensworth.

"Yes, it is all done," he said to her. "The doctor was quite unsurprised that it should have happened—he had been expecting it for some time."

"Well, never mind about that now," interrupted Lady Lingdale firmly. "Now you are here, Ravensworth, perhaps you will talk a little sense into these two young people. Here is Theodora, vowing she will not take a penny from the old man should he have left his fortune to her, and Edmund encouraging her! And they are saying they do not mean to marry, after all!"

"It grieves me to disappoint you, Cousin Amelia," said Ravensworth, bowing with negligent grace over the hand that she proffered him distractedly, "but I am afraid I am unable to do as you ask."

"Unable? Whatever do you mean?"

"It has been brought to my notice that I have been interfering far too much in my ward's private life," he informed her suavely, with a lift of his eyebrow, unseen by her ladyship, towards Theodora.

"Interfering? I do not understand you. Of course Edmund is most grateful for your care. I am sure he would never be such a monster of ingratitude as to say anything of the sort. Tell your cousin, Edmund!"

Edmund opened his mouth, and closed it again.

"Come on, Edmund!" encouraged Ravensworth. "Are you grateful to me for arranging for you to go hunting, and shooting, and for introducing you to my club?"

"No! That is, yes, I am. Dash it, Ravensworth, I am grateful that you did so, for I realise now that you meant well by me. But I should tell you that I do not like hunting or shooting, and never have! As for your club—but perhaps we won't talk about that just now."

"You may be right," his guardian said in answer to his imploring look, "though I must tell you I am only too happy to accept the consequences of that particular piece of folly! However, that is quite beside the point. Now do you see, Amelia? Edmund is a man now, and it is not for me to do more than advise him."

"Do so, then!" almost shrieked Lady Lingdale. "And, while you are at it, advise this foolish girl that she cannot fly in the face of providence, and turn down such a legacy! She says she will not accept it, and also that she will not marry Edmund either! I shall go distracted!"

"Do you want her to marry him, if she is not to inherit?" he asked with the air of one studying some new and interesting phenomenon.

"No, I suppose not, though to be sure I am—at least I was—very fond of the child, and I thought Edmund cared for her, though they say it is not so. But to break it off now, when it is just about to be known that she will have nothing—it is not to be thought of! Whatever will people say?"

"It does not matter what they say," he said carelessly. "I informed Theodora, some time ago, that under no circumstances would I permit her to marry my ward."

"You did what?" exploded Edmund. "Of all the high-handed, interfering, damnable..." He encountered a look of such blazing fury from Theodora that the words died in

his throat. Mouth open, he gazed at her, and then at his
guardian, who was watching her with a look on his face
that he had never seen before. "So that's it! You sly devil,
Ravensworth!" He advanced and took Theodora's hand,
lifting her to her feet so that he might embrace her heart-
ily. After a painful hug he lifted her hand to his lips, then
held it out to his cousin. "It was never mine, you know,
but I take the liberty of giving it to you anyway," he said.

"Very prettily done," approved his guardian. "I can see
that your education has proceeded apace." And under
Lady Lingdale's affronted gaze he took Theodora into his
arms, and proceeded to kiss her with great thoroughness
and deliberation. She struggled for a moment, and her ladyship held her breath, expecting and indeed hoping for an
outburst of maidenly modesty, but Theodora's only wish
was to have her arms free, so that she might clasp them
round Ravensworth's neck and return his caresses with
such abandon that Lady Lingdale was outraged.

"Theodora! Ravensworth! Kindly cease this unseemly
behaviour!"

Her protests were ignored. Edmund gave a crack of
laughter, and went to take her arm.

"Come along, Mama. They do not heed you, you
know! We had better leave them alone for a while."

"Alone? I never heard of anything so shocking! Or saw,
for that matter!"

"Then the sooner you come away, the less you will see.
Now don't argue with me, Mama. You are overwrought; I
will take you to your dressing-room, and tell your maid to
give you some of your drops."

In the newly masterful manner he had just acquired he
drew her from the room. Mesmerised, she allowed herself
to be led away and, before she could find the words to argue, she was lying on the couch in her dressing-room, and

the maid was fussing over her. Her look of dismay was almost comical.

"Edmund..."

"Don't worry, Mama. I will stay with you, and we will have a nice cosy chat when you have taken your drops. There! Now you will soon feel much more the thing. You are not going to make a fuss, are you, Mama?"

"No, Edmund," she said meekly. "But it does seem a waste, when he is so rich already..."

"Now not another word," he said. "You may be quite sure that she would never have consented to keep any money from that man. It is fortunate that Cousin Alexander need not mind that she will have so small a fortune. And think how fortunate it is that he should marry someone we both like so much! We shall all be good friends!"

Much struck, Lady Lingdale pondered these wise words. The vision of what might have been, had Alexander married some haughty Society heiress, passed through her mind. Such a woman would have had little time for impecunious relations, and once Edmund came of age would probably have seen to it that her husband did little or nothing for his cousins.

"You are very right, dear," she said. Edmund gave a satisfied smile, and patted her hand.

In the drawing-room, Theodora and Ravensworth were now sitting on a sofa. Theodora leaned back against the cushions, her eyes bright as she looked at Alexander, who was carefully kissing each of her fingers in turn before turning her hand over and pressing his lips to her palm. The kisses, soft and yet fiery, travelled up her arm, tasting the baby-soft skin inside her elbow and the smooth rounding of her shoulder from which he slipped the neckline of her dress. Since the Princess's party had been intended to last all evening, she had not veiled the low-cut bodice with a fichu, as was usual for day wear, and now she shivered as, with fingers and lips, he caressed her neck and the soft rise of her breasts. Reaching the little hollow at the base of her throat, he could feel her heartbeat, rapid and strong, and raised his head to look at her.

"How fast your heart is beating," he said wonderingly. "You are not frightened of me, are you?"

"Frightened? No, never," she replied softly, tracing with her fingertips the line of his eyebrows, and smoothing away the little frown that had appeared between them.

"I could never do anything to hurt you, Theodora. I love you far too much."

She smiled at him mistily. "You haven't said that before," she said shyly.

"Haven't I? What a shockingly remiss lover I am. To think that I always prided myself on my address! The truth is, I was never in earnest before, and to feel like this is as new to me as it is to you. I feel as gauche as Edmund, and it occurs to me that I have not even proposed to you! How very fast of you, love, to let me take such liberties!"

He would have withdrawn from her embrace to go down on his knees and make his proposal in form, but she would not let him.

"There is no need," she said simply. "I was always yours, from the first moment when you kissed me."

After that, she was unable to speak for quite some time; nor would she have wished to. Edmund, putting his head quietly round the door, withdrew with a smile. They did not notice him at all.

HARLEQUIN ROMANCE®

Harlequin Romance
knows that lasting love
is something special . . .

And so is
next month's
title in

THE BRIDAL COLLECTION

TEMPORARY ARRANGEMENT
by Shannon Waverly

THE BRIDE was an unwelcome guest.
THE GROOM was a reluctant host.
The arrangement was *supposed*
to be temporary but—
THE WEDDING made it for keeps!

Available this month in
The Bridal Collection
RESCUED BY LOVE
by Anne Marie Duquette #3253

Wherever Harlequin books are sold.

Where do you find hot Texas nights, smooth Texas charm and dangerously sexy cowboys?

COWBOYS AND CABERNET

Raise a glass—Texas style!

Tyler McKinney is out to prove a Texas ranch is the perfect place for a vineyard. Vintner Ruth Holden thinks Tyler is too stubborn, too impatient, too…Texas. And far too difficult to resist!

CRYSTAL CREEK reverberates with the exciting rhythm of Texas. Each story features the rugged individuals who live and love in the Lone Star State. And each one ends with the same invitation…

Y'ALL COME BACK…REAL SOON!

Don't miss *COWBOYS AND CABERNET* by Margot Dalton. Available in April wherever Harlequin books are sold.
